RAY VS THE
MEANING OF LIFE

Michael F. Stewart

RAY VS THE MEANING OF LIFE

By Michael F. Stewart

Copyright 2018 Michael F. Stewart
Cover Art by Martin Stiff
Formatting by Polgarus Studio

www.michaelfstewart.com

For Teagan and Natasha.

Chapter 1

Here's what killed Grandma:

The garbage truck pulled into Sunny Days RV Park at half past nine. I was gaming in my camper and missed most of it, but there were witnesses. Grandma was checking on the trailers like she did every morning to make sure no one was "cavorting."

Now my half-sister, Crystal, she was hunting with her rifle out. The .22, for picking off squirrels, even the odd raccoon, you know . . . *dinner*. But Crystal didn't kill Grandma. She says Grandma's dying was the same as one of those domino setups, where one thing follows another.

The truck roared up from the main gate in a direct line headed to the rear, where the garbage was piled. It'd been raining, and mud pooled in the road's tire ruts.

The way Crystal tells it, she hit that squirrel with the crack of a rifle shot. The bullet knocked it from the tree branch and onto the face of Grandma, who staggered, screeching, into the path of the truck. The truck locked its wheels and slid through the mud like a greased pig through a farmer's fingers.

But the truck didn't kill Grandma.

My ma, who had been scrubbing toilets, lurched out of the stalls, bucket sloshing, and witnessed what came next. Says that getting squished by the truck would've been better. One of those dream catchers people use to keep away nightmares hung in the truck's windscreen. Grandma had a weird fear of dream catchers. Seeing the feathers dangling from the web of gut, she screamed and ran toward the garbage pile.

Near the bins, smoke was streaming from Uncle Jamie's firework shack. He was doing what he's always doing, mixing various powders and such to concoct his explosions. The whole shack looks like it's ready to fall over; he just leans the metal sheets together like walls. Says it's not laziness, but to release pressure in the event of what happens all the time.

In my game, I was protecting a party of rangers, hacking dragon spawn left and right. My trailer's back in the woods, nearer to Uncle Jamie's than anyone else's, and atop a tiny hill to keep it out of the swamp and to improve reception. But this is what I heard happened from those witnesses: Grandma was sprinting, which is a little like a dog with two legs, a front right one and a rear left, trying to run. And smoke was a pouring, and the truck was a roaring and chasing Grandma like a nightmare itself, when Uncle added the wrong powder and . . .

KABOOM!

But the fireworks didn't kill Grandma, either.

Tina witnessed all the rest—Tina's pretty much the smartest, most beautiful girl in the universe; just a glance from her and I can walk on top of all this mud, know what I mean? She's the reason why I, at the age of seventeen, keep flipping burgers at the park's burger joint where she works with her dad, instead of doing the famous stuff I'm meant to do. Now Tina says the firework shack went off like an exploding unicorn, all rainbows and sparkles. Uncle Jamie was fine, never had hair anyways, except on his buttocks; the man's buttocks are as hairy as a bear's, which is a great segue because . . .

The blast shook me from my game, but it shoved Grandma to her knees. She shouted about cavalry and artillery. Tina screamed, "Bear!" Grandma crawled for cover, right into the woods. Mom said Grandma headed for me, that I could have helped her more, but I don't know how. I wish I could've— really, I do. But Tina says the bear had been waiting.

Bears don't usually do that. Wait, I mean. They come around before the garbage truck because they like to pick through the refuse, but usually black bears, not grizzlies like this monster. It's a bad thing when a bear starts stalking.

While Grandma crawled, Uncle Jamie stumbled around in a daze. Mom says the smoke hit her then. But the bear was freaked out by all the noise.

This next bit I'll never forget, because I was there.

After the blast, I snatched a climbing hammer—closest thing to me—and a can of bear spray, and bolted out the door. I hollered, still too far away to use the spray, and sprinted through spiny pine branches that snagged on my bare chest.

Coat pearly in the sun and as big as a trailer itself, the bear towered on thick haunches. Grandma gave it this puggish scowl and shook her head at the thing. That's when the bear hugged Grandma the way she hated to be hugged. Her spine snapped like a branch in a storm.

As I broke into the clearing, I could tell Grandma was a

goner. She hung over the bear's leg like a towel on a rack. Tears blurred my vision, but you didn't need to see well to use bear spray. I knelt and aimed between its shoulder blades.

The grizzly dropped Grandma to spring's frost-bitten leaves and bumbled off, leaving her crumpled on the ground.

The bear's what killed Grandma, or so everyone thinks. And life won't ever be the same.

Chapter 2

I'm first to her side. Her eyes are staring. "Dead," I whisper, with my fingers at Grandma's wrist and my heart pounding as if to make up for hers. "Grandma, no."

A rifle shot cracks. Tree bark splinters near my head.

"Sorry," Crystal shouts. "Thought you was another bear. Get a haircut."

"Sheeit," my mom says. "Call the freezer people."

I glower at my ma. Grandma was rich. She owned Sunny Days RV Park and wasn't all that pleased about getting old, so she'd arranged for the freezer people to come and freeze her if by chance she kicked it. Grandma always told everyone her Last Will and Testament would be a "doozy." "You can take my park, but I'm gonna want it back when I resurrect like Jesus," she'd say.

Uncle Jamie sobs, tears plowing through soot, leaving muddy streaks. I quake, wearing nothing more than my undies and my boots, too stunned to do more than gawk.

Within three minutes of that bear attack, a steady whomping sound begins, coming from the direction of Big Mountain, and moments later a speck of silver near the snowcapped peak flashes in the morning sun. My climbing hammer's cold in my palm, two years old and still shiny as the day I bought it. I'd planned to set out to climb the Big today—that will have to wait, like it had to wait yesterday and every day of the last year and the year before.

We gape as the silver speck grows. None of us has ever seen a helicopter this large. It lands, taking up six empty trailer slabs. A dozen figures pour out, clad in head-to-toe coveralls and masks as if we might be zombies.

"How'd they know?" Ma asks the question I'm thinking.

"App," Tina says, slouchy eyes serious. "There's an app for everything now."

The door of the helicopter reads: TIMELY CRYOGENICS— DON'T MISS A BEAT. NOW ON ANDROID!

"Is this Madame Georgia Saintbury?" The man spoke from within a sealed helmet.

"Madame," Mom snickers.

"Yep," I say.

"Don't think you can just pick up a dead—" It's Tina, and she's taking pictures. A dozen hands heft an old woman who probably weighs all of a hundred pounds on account of the dwindles, and they carry her like Gandhi through the door of the helicopter.

We all walk with them, boots squelching, but they don't let us in. She's laid on a table in the belly of the ship. Someone runs a circular saw as the rear hatch slowly closes.

"They're not going to . . . what I think they're going to . . . ," Tina whispers.

Mom says, "Freezer people. Wait a second . . ." And she bangs on the ship and shouts, "Hey! How much this all costing?"

"Grandma's dime," Uncle says, and Mom whirls on him like a snake strike.

"She's dead, Jamie—that money's ours now."

Uncle Jamie backs up a step.

The freezer people take an hour. I stand in the mud, listening to sawing and shouting inside, feeling a little like Grandma's been abducted by aliens and she'll step out of there smiling but with dead eyes. Tina offers me a coffee and I take it, but really only so I can hold something she held. In my head I keep hearing the crack of Grandma's spine.

Doc Kingfish, the local family doctor who also works as the coroner, arrives, but he's not allowed into the ship until they walk out hefting what looks like a slow cooker. Frost ghosts from the lid and coats the stainless steel. The alien-guy holds it out wearing gloves. A cord dangles from the bottom. "Need to plug this in," he says. "Quick."

"She didn't pay for storage?" Tina asks.

The sides are so cold they burn, and I grab two of Ma's cleaning rags for my palms to hold it.

"Is it . . .?" Tina asks, reaching out but not touching the container.

"Madame Georgia Saintbury," alien-guy says. "The important part. Don't forget to plug her in."

It's not all of her; in this canister floats my grandma's brain. It's no accident that I'm the one holding it. Other than Uncle Jamie, I'm probably the only soul in the park who thinks it's worth keeping, with the exception of Grandma herself.

I carry it to the spot she's prepared for it: a giant, fiberglass version of herself. The park mascot. She had it made ten years ago and has been talking about her immortality ever since, drinking champagne and eating caviar just to get a rise from her daughter. Twelve feet tall, with each breast the size of my head, it's more Barbie doll than Grandma, but she insists it's how she looked before gravity struck.

Two generators in a concrete shell beneath her feet will fire up if the power ever goes out, which it does a lot here. On a stepladder, I slide the brain into the back of Grandma's head and pull on the cord. It's three feet too short. "Anyone have an extension? For Grandma's brain?" I shout.

No one answers.

"I need a brain extension," I call. "Chrissake."

From one trailer come snorts of laughter. It's somehow contagious because, as Grandma defrosts, Tina giggles and Mom's yelling where she stands over the body bag the aliens are leaving behind. I manage to laugh through some tears. But no one has a cord, so I slog through the mud toward my trailer. The helicopter sends leaves swirling and disappears like it's never been.

My door thwacks against the trailer's side, and my eyes water at the smell, a mix of mac-and-cheese and sour laundry. After a moment, my eyes and nose acclimatize. One bed, an ultra-tiny kitchen with a bar fridge and hot plate and sink, and a table designed for two but reconfigured for my multiscreen computer rig. Beside the table are piled loops of rope, carabiners, and a bag of chalk—everything I need to climb the Big, to figure out what I'm supposed to do in life, you know?—but gaming's been keeping me busy.

I drop the hammer in the pile. My thumb's nearly on the computer's power button to wake it before I remember Grandma and dip down to pull up the nest of cabling, yanking the plugs from their seats and heading back out into a now-warming day with the power strip. A minute later Grandma's on the grid.

A light on the front of the steel canister goes green with lots of bars. "There you are, Grandma," I say. "Sorry." I swallow down a thick paste of guilt. "Sorry I wasn't there. Only playing my games . . . You comfortable?"

The unit hums in reply. I scrape a sad face into the frost before walking back to Doc Kingfish, a man who knows more than anyone about everyone in town.

Doc's leaning over a long black bag with Tina.

"Someone's gone and taken the brain," he says. "Cause of death."

"That's not what killed her," Tina says, pointing at Big Mountain, though the helicopter has already disappeared behind its peak. "*They* just did that."

"Then maybe the—"

"The broken back, maybe the broken back," Tina replies, gripping her forehead. "From when the grizzly was squeezing her?"

Even now, even with my grandma dead at her feet, Tina's this bright light for me. I'm not sure how I'll convince her that I'm *her* light, but that's my plan this summer, before it's too late.

"The broken back. That's what I was gonna say." Doc meets my eye. "Hey, Ray, Pulled Beef open yet?"

I'd been staring at Tina and jerk away. Pulled Beef is the park's burger joint, owned by Tina's father, Salminder. If Tina's the light guiding me home, then her father's always been a safe harbor. They arrived to open the restaurant a week ago, as they have every spring. It's where I spend most my summer flipping burgers.

"His grandma's dead. Ray can't be cooking," Tina says. I just stand there, suddenly flushing at my lack of clothes. Red welts crisscross my chest and stomach from when I fought through the pine trees.

"No, I'll do it," I say. "People still gotta eat. Just have to clean up and dress first."

As I head to the washrooms, I pass my mom. She's yelling at Grandma's brain and threatening to unplug her.

"You'd better have done right by me!" her shout echoes back from the Big.

I jump at Crystal's sudden snarl behind me. "That bear's a man-killer, won't stop now," Crystal says. A powerful, scoped rifle is strapped to her back and a jar's worth of camo-paint is smeared over her face. She shoves me out of the way. Black army boots trounce through the muck. "Gonna kill that bear before it kills again. That's what's right."

Right. As if anyone can know what's really right. But as she clumps into the thick woods, I can't help a stab of jealousy. She has something she can do. A purpose. I wonder if she feels guilty about the squirrel, like she started it all, but I say nothing.

I say nothing because I know what *really* started it all. Last night Grandma and I pulled an all-nighter playing *Arcane Dynasty*. This morning, she'd huffed off after I killed her onscreen by accident, collateral damage in a fireball spell.

In the washroom, I splash water on my face to hide all the

tears that keep coming. Right before the squirrel, the truck, the dream catcher, the explosion, and the bear, there was Ray. I was the first domino.

Grandma's dead, and I killed her.

Chapter 3

Mom's gone off with Doc. They want me to grill them a hamburger brunch. With Grandma's brain watching from the statue, I'm not quite ready to handle more frozen meat.

Uncle Jamie's left staring at the body bag, tears dripping from his nose.

"Wanna move her somewhere?" I ask.

He nods at the bag.

I go and stand at what I hope are the feet. Uncle Jamie slowly moves to pull the other end out of the mud. There's a sucking sound, and then we hold her sagging body bag between us.

The walls of Uncle Jamie's shack are lying on the ground, leaving only a tin roof and four spindly posts. Official opening day's not until tomorrow, so only three of the camper slabs are occupied, and none of the rental trailers, but Mom won't want a body in one of those. This far north, ghost stories linger and scare away customers.

"You could put her in mine," I say, cringing. "Funeral won't be long, right? The undertaker will be here soon to pick her up?"

He nods again and we shuffle slowly to my trailer, following a winding trail upward over a root-snarled path. I'm regretting not stopping at the showers to wash the mud off the bag. As he opens the door, Uncle Jamie winces at the smell, but backs up the stairs. On the count of three, we heave her onto my bed.

He stares down at her. "Needs fresh air," he says.

Uncle Jamie unzips the top. I wish he hadn't done that. She's gone chalk white and, where the zipper has pressed, there's a bruised trail like someone's biked across her face. Stitches crown her forehead. "Gotta . . . ," I croak, but Uncle Jamie doesn't even look up as I burst from the trailer to rest my hands on my knees and breathe. Again I'm jealous of Crystal, out there in the woods, on a mission while I want nothing more than to vomit. I have to get out of this campground, but it lies fifty miles north of the nearest small town and three hundred to the closest real city. I've got nowhere to go.

As I march toward Pulled Beef, on the far side of the campground, I cut through empty lots and across trailer "slabs"—called that because of the hunks of concrete that delineate one site from another—each with their own electrical outlet and a fire pit. The campground can hold a hundred RVs and as many tents as campers can find a dry patch. The muddy road follows an S-shape through the park. I'm not really sure how far back it goes; there's no fence or anything, just keeps on through birch and pine-spotted swamp to Big Mountain. I pass the rusty play structures and a leaf-carpeted pool. My mom keeps reminding me to open the pool despite the iceberg floating in it. I can hear her and Doc talking as I close on the patio.

"We don't need a burial or nothing," my mom says. "The freezer people was what she wanted."

Doc explains, "The executor will read the will, and that'll tell you what Georgia wanted. Surely, she left something for her funeral."

"Don't need a funeral if no one's going to come to it. Besides, you don't get two special things when you die. You get one. She picked brain freezing. Two is . . . gratuitous." I'm creeping up, trying to keep my boots quiet, but I can see she looks pleased with her word choice.

"The executor carries out the wishes. They control the process, but the will tells it like it is . . . Your ma gets final say." Doc swallows as if embarrassed. "What . . . uh . . . what do you think you'll do with a million dollars anyways?"

"A million dollars, you really think?" my mom asks Doc in a way that says she's been counting the money for a decade.

"Sure I do. Plain old land has gone for that near here, let alone a fully operating business. I'm on the Town Council, you know? We'd put your name in lights if you'd donate—"

"Mom will want me to keep the park for her, so she can take it back when she thaws." Doc gives her a searching look, and they both break into laughter. "Naw . . . Always wanted to travel, I have. A big new trailer maybe, and—" Her wistful eyes settle on mine, narrowing. She smiles with a smarm she reserves only for me. It never reaches her eyes. It's sweet and sour at the same time, like Chinese chicken balls covered in syrupy red sauce. "Kids' education's important too, isn't it, Ray? Crystal might want to go to college for something."

I'm pretty sure if Crystal came into money she'd just buy bigger guns. "I could go to college?"

"You remember who let you borrow that trailer of yours, don't you, hun?"

I stuff my hands into the pockets of my jeans. "What do you mean?"

"The trailer where you sleep. The one you got after you decided you were too good to help around the park so much."

I swallow. Grandma is resting in my bed now.

And it hits me like a tree no one saw falling. *Snap.* My grandma was the only thing that kept me in my trailer. When I left home, my mom told me in no uncertain terms—*when Grandma's gone, you is gone.* Now that'll happen whether my mom goes and sells the park or not. I shudder at the thought of staying as much as the thought of going. I'd rather not think about any of it at all. "She's still warm, Mom. Grandma's still warm."

Her face screws up. "Never was, Ray. Never was. Now get on that grill and no more video games."

"I wasn't playing—and I have dozens of people watching me play . . ." But it's no use, she's turned back to Doc.

"When can I get the will?" she asks.

"I'll send a note off to the lawyer, and she won't make you wait on it. You'll have the will tonight."

Grandma's fiberglass head pokes above a trailer roof. In the morning sun, its shadow stretches clear across the patio.

Pulled Beef is an ancient Winnebago with a hole cut in the side that opens to become a food counter. Inside's all set up like a kitchen. Although it's on wheels, the tires sagged long ago and the rims are sunken so deep in the ground that the trailer almost rests on the chassis. A chalkboard menu has one thing written on it.

Burger $5.

The door's unlocked.

After I shut it, I lean against the steel frame, the whole trailer squealing beneath my weight, and bite my lip. Salminder stands there, giant bulb of his sky-blue headgear nodding, smile like a searchlight, even nearly buried in a wiry beard shot through with gray.

"I'm sorry about Grandma Georgia," he says and embraces me. I'm like a sapling whereas he's a wide tree stump, so my chin rests in his turban. "Tina told me."

He doesn't have to be here. Grandma had never been nice to him. Probably because he took over the camp cooking when she stopped baking her apple pies. Pies, burgers, all the same to me, but Grandma never ate a burger. Not a one.

"I'll miss Grandma," I say, leaving unspoken that no one else except Uncle Jamie will.

"She seemed happy."

"Yeah, happy as a crow picking apart a fish head."

"A person's life is long and the ending of it doesn't tell the tale. Unfortunately, it is what we most remember," Salminder says.

"New diet?" Even with the beard I can tell he's lost weight.

"Wouldn't wish it on anyone," he says and begins unwrapping the stainless-steel bins of condiments as I fetch beef patties from the chest freezer. The steel and meat remind me of Grandma's brain, and I'm really struggling to hold everything down. It's barely eleven o'clock. Grandma's dead. Her brainless corpse is lying on my bed. Mom's counting her money. And I have to figure out where I'm going to sleep when I get kicked out. But, if I shut my eyes, all I see is the image of Grandma's dead video game avatar burned into my retinas.

The grill ignites with a thump. I open the counter window, ready to smile at my customers. I doubt very much that the smile reaches my eyes.

Chapter 4

We all know why we're around the bonfire. Wood crackles and pops. White smoke always seems to blow in my direction, but it can't force me from Tina's side. Maybe if it had been a funeral pyre like my mom wanted, but the doc said it was illegal to burn a body or to bury it ourselves. I'd been hopeful. In my trailer, dead Grandma smell is overtaking Kraft Dinner odor. Mom decided she could wait for the undertaker—after all, what's a few thousand dollars when she'd soon inherit a million?—but she avoided my questions about when the undertaker would arrive.

That's what I'm waiting on, but everyone else awaits the will. The lawyer said she'd drive it up from town, that's a good hour, and it's been at least that. Salminder's here with Tina, her hair the color of molasses and shining with the moon. She's sixteen now. With her being a year behind me, I don't see Tina around school much, but the gap in our ages has somehow narrowed since last summer. Then she was all braces and gangly limbs; now she's grown into herself. My body's taking its sweet time. Until recently I'd always seen us as equals, but now . . . she's leveled up. I should have told her how I felt about her long, long ago.

Uncle hasn't washed since the explosion and sits silent, throwing tiny packets of powder into the fire. They fizzle and flare, some copper-green, others magnesium-white. In the chill, we all huddle too close to the flames, sipping hot chocolate and Mom, her whiskey. Crystal's still on the bear's trail, but everyone else's here, even some rare park tourists—a couple from Montana who speak with a twang, and a pair of newlyweds starting everything off wrong with a dead grandma in a muddy RV park. The man keeps sobbing as though it was his relative in my bed. At least they don't need to worry about Grandma stopping their cavorting.

Mom smiles and her eyes shine. "Remember how Grandma didn't like to waste nothing?" She looks around and comes to stare at her brother. "Remember, Jamie, how she used to pick mushrooms in the forest, cook 'em up and watch us eat to see if she should, too?"

Uncle Jamie shakes his head. "Wasn't like that. She jes' wanted to make sure we was full first. Brought home a whole deer once though." He slaps his knee. "Now that was something. Found it on the side of the road."

"Liked her food, that one," Mom adds. "Surprised the bear got her. Remember the turkey?"

Uncle Jamie snorts, and they smile at one another, sharing the joke before coming 'round to tell us. I've heard this story a dozen times if I've heard it once.

"Thanksgiving, ten years ago now," Mom says, face turning up to the stars in recollection. "We was letting the turkey thaw on the trailer counter when some hungry little black bear gone and let itself in. Grandma was having a nap. When she woke and hollered, the bear took the whole bird and skedaddled. I was just washing up when the trailer door opened. First out came the bear thief, and then Grandma naked as a babe—flying. She jumped the steps and landed on the bear's back. Never knew a bear could make that sound. Squealed like a pig."

"Grandma tackled a bear?" Tina asked. "Naked?"

"Liked her food," Mom replies. "Got the turkey back."

"Grizzly, the bear that got her," Uncle Jamie says quietly. "No grandma's a match for a grizzly."

"'Twas like the woman was missing this part of her brain," Doc says, tapping his frontal lobe. "If you don't mind my saying."

I pat him on the shoulder, letting him know it's okay.

"Told the truth," Uncle Jamie agrees. "Knew where you stood with a mother like that."

"Her nickname for me was RB. 'Ray the Bastard,'" I say. "I liked that."

"Good pie, too," Mom says, "Tough, mean old bird, though. Weren't you, Ma?"

Half of us check over our shoulders to peer at Grandma's brain, but the firelight doesn't reach that far.

That sucked the life from the conversation, and only the pop and hiss of escaping water breaks the silence until headlights weave down the drive. The shiny new pickup truck slides to a stop, but the driver leaves the engine on. Sam Peregrine, wearing a beige pantsuit, steps onto the glowing running board of her truck and sniffs. She pauses to glance down at the mud and then hops to a drier patch. A bundle of manila envelopes is stuck in her armpit.

"'Bout time," my mom says loud enough.

Without a word, Sam Peregrine hands an envelope each to my mom, my uncle, and me, and then peers around. "Crystal's off hunting," I say, and Sam Peregrine's head bobs.

"Aren't you going to read it to us?" Uncle Jamie asks.

Sam smiles. "They just do that for movies and books."

"Don't want her reading," Mom says. "Charges by the minute that one."

They squint at one another.

"Those are copies of Georgia Saintbury's Last Will and Testament," Sam Peregrine says. "The original has been filed with the court and everything's legit. I am trustee, and executor. If you have questions about the estate, we can get to them when I'm back from my holidays."

"Would you like to stay for a tea?" Uncle asks.

Sam Peregrine's puckered beak unfurls into a smile. "Thanks, Jamie—"

"Not a two hundred dollar tea, you won't." My mom and the lawyer return to squints.

Before Sam Peregrine turns away, smug satisfaction spreads across her face. It might have been a trick of the firelight, but I swear she winked at me.

Tina leans in toward my envelope. I catch the furrow between her eyebrows. It's not only my life being decided tonight, it's hers too. If Grandma's park gets sold, Pulled Beef gets sold along with it. I'm more interested in the press of Tina's shoulder on mine.

Mom wrestles with her seal. Uncle Jamie sits sadly, taking his time with his letter. I can't think for the smell of Tina's hair; it's like lilacs in full bloom. I just hold my copy, surprised I have anything to open at all, but knowing I must be named somewhere in the will.

My mom's eyes first widen and then they narrow, starting back over at the top of the page. As she reads, her shoulders keep riding up toward her ears. Uncle Jamie twists so that the firelight shines on his copy. Sam Peregrine's already back in her truck and turning it around.

My mom starts screaming. "No, no, no! That bitch, *that bitch*!" And then she's scrambling toward Sam Peregrine's red taillights. As the truck disappears along the winding, tree-shrouded drive, Mom veers toward the statue of Grandma.

"Oh no," I say, and I'm scrambling after her because I'm guessing what she's planning to do, but when she glances over her shoulder and sees me, she stops, lifts the envelope like it's a hatchet, and starts yelling.

"You bastard, you bastard!"

And I have no idea what I've gone and done this time.

Chapter 5

I skid in the muck, arms out for balance, coming to a stop between her and the campfire. "What are you talking about, Mom?"

She stands, face red from the glow of the flames, and hatchet chops the will at me. Grandma looms dark and busty at her back. I turn to Uncle, but his pages fold limp over his hands and he stares, as if I might be more than I seem.

"Fire," Mom gasps. She holds the will out as she races forward to plunge the pages into the flames, smiles crazily as they catch, and then shrieks when she sees Uncle's will and grabs it, flinging the papers into the fire where they too ignite. She cackles until her gaze burns on me and my envelope.

I twist and sprint, skating in the mud.

"Muriel!" It's my uncle shouting for my mother. "It don't matter."

But I hear her huffing close behind. She's strong; decades of cleaning trailers and washrooms has given her a special kind of fitness. The will's crumpled and muddy in my fingers. I'm running for my trailer. After hundreds of nighttime bathroom trips, I know every root along my path and my mom stumbles as I fly, hit the trailer, and open the door to such putrescence that I fall back. My mother's there, ready to grapple me.

Something big rustles at the edge of the forest. "Bear!" I cry before I can filter everything that's happening.

"What's he done?" a voice asks from the tree line.

Mom fumbles for the bear spray she keeps clipped to her belt.

The figure moves closer and levels a gun barrel at my chest. I see the face. Crystal's pointed chin and curled lip stick out.

"Crystal," I say. "Scared the heck—"

"What's he gone and done?" she asks again, the gun moving steadily closer. She doesn't often miss, and from this range missing isn't possible.

"Lower the gun, Crystal. Come on now," I say.

"The will, he has the will." Mom points to me.

Crystal sidesteps hunter-like into the trailer's clearing and snatches the will from my outstretched hand. With the gunstock tucked into her armpit, she tears the envelope open and brings it close to her face in the low light.

She only reads a moment. Crystal's not the quickest of readers but, whatever she read, it's enough. The will slips to the pine needles. The gun barrel lifts. "Didn't he just cry about a bear?" she asks.

I frown, not understanding.

"Bear!" she shouts. "Right, Mama?"

"What are you talking about?" I yell back.

I catch the alarmed squeaks of the newlyweds.

"You see a bear? Tough to tell in the dark, right? Mistakes happen," Crystal says without inflection.

"Oh—" My mom covers her mouth.

"I'm not a bear. It's me! Ray!" Cold panic rolls over my chest as I scream. "Help!"

Crystal's waiting for my mother's signal.

There's a moment, too long of one, before my mother's shoulders sag, and she shakes her head.

"Don't." Uncle Jamie's on the trail. "It don't matter."

The gun barrel drops a foot, and I swallow. "What does the will say?" I ask. "Tell me."

"Says my park's yours," my mom replies and then hocks spit onto the ground.

"The park . . . ," I say. "Sunny Days?"

"All of it," she says. "Yours."

"Don't make any sense." Crystal's fingers twitch around the gun trigger. "You never did nothing but flip burgers."

"There has to be a mistake," I say, agreeing with them. I tiptoe over to Crystal and pinch the will from the ground without taking my eyes from her.

Then I read.

Dear Living Folks,

If you're reading this, then I have been temporarily inconvenienced by what is presently known as the condition of 'death.' When I am resurrected these here papers will be null and void and I get everything back. That's the deal. Until then this is what I'm thinking. Since the lawyering says I have to give it to someones, I'm thinking that none of yous have done nothing with your lives and yous gonna lose me my investment. Muriel and James, it's too late for you. And Crystal—you too, the way you're headed. So, to ensure there's something left over when I am thawed out, I'm doing this:

This is my Last Will and Testement.

To my daughter, Muriel Saintbury, I leave nothing 'cept my tea set and my dentures—I'll have real teeth in the future.

To my son, James Saintbury, I leave nothing save my book collection. Maybe you'll learn to read better than me.

To my granddaughter, Crystal Saintbury, I leave nothing 'cept my truck. You'll need it to pack up your ma and uncle and git. I'll get a flying truck when I return.

To my grandson, Raymond Saintbury, I leave everything else. You don't have much of a chance, but we'll see if you pass the test.*

The page goes on to list "everything else." The trailers, the sheds, my mom's trailer, Uncle's, and the land—there's more of that than I'd figured.

To my grandson, Raymond Saintbury, I leave everything else.

But I'm just looking for the little asterisk and what it means. It's two pages in.

*To be confirmed. If at the end of one month Ray can tell Sam Peregrine the meaning of life—see sealed letter for correct answer—he gets everything. ** If he fails, then he gets nothing and my children split the rest. Until such time as I is given a new body. One of you might go and surprise me.

"Didn't any of you read the whole thing?" I ask.

"The part where you get everything?" Mom asks. "Yeah, I caught that."

"Only if I can figure out the meaning of life!" I say. I start scanning the note to find the meaning of the double asterisks I spotted.

"See—don't matter," Uncle Jamie says, and it would have been nice if he had explained what he meant a little earlier.

Mom snatches the will back from me, digs into her pocket, and snaps on a flashlight.

After a minute she starts flicking the pages with her fingers. She smiles with not only her mouth, but also her eyes, nose, ears—even her neck wrinkles grin. "Ha!" she shouts and then knuckles me in the shoulder. "As if, right? As if, huh? Put that gun down, Crystal, you'll go to jail."

"So he doesn't get it?" Crystal asks.

"Nope, gets it only if he tells Sam Peregrine the meaning of life."

Crystal's face screws and then slowly relaxes.

"What's the double star mean, the asterisks?" I ask.

Mom studies the will for a minute before folding it back away. "Don't you worry about that, won't make a difference anyways."

I catch her glare and turn to Uncle Jamie.

"Don't look at me," he says. "I didn't get to any double asterisks before Muriel went and burned my copy."

My mom backs away as I approach with my hand out, and she stuffs the will into her bra, from which I've never seen anything return except a seemingly endless supply of Kleenex.

"What's the meaning of life, Ray?" Crystal laughs. "Video games?"

"Wrong answer, Crys," Mom replies. "The will says life, not virtual life."

They both laugh.

I flush red. I have no idea what the meaning of life might be, but as they walk off with the will, laughing away, I really wish I knew. I wish, but I don't even know where to start. What I do know, having seen the whites of all their crazed eyes, is I need to get out of Sunny Days or it will be too late for me to figure anything out.

One way or another, it's Ray versus the meaning of life, now.

Chapter 6

It'll be a long night with Grandma in my trailer. Everyone else goes back to the fire, all shouting mean laughter and poking fun and sparks into the night. Noise carries out here. They took my will with them, and I never did figure out what came with the double asterisks. Without the cable I used to plug Grandma in, I can't even go online to search for the meaning of life.

There's a small part of me that floats on the ceiling. The trailer park. A million dollars. It's mine? A million dollars is too big of a number for me to conceive of.

Grandma's still on my bed in her body bag, wearing a nightgown. Her wiry gray hair is teased out. I have her hair, all crazy curls, but mine's mud brown. She's tough to look at. Rigor mortis has set in and her arms have curled at the elbows to stretch out like a zombie waiter or something. I try to push them down, but they're stiff and the hands cold and bone-white. My trailer's so small that I have to lie down beside her to sleep. I pull the blanket to my chin and then I pull it to hers too.

Sleep doesn't come.

Critters rustle about in the leaves and ramble across my

rooftop. I can hear the leaves fall and the crackle of the fire even though it's down near the office. My office. But that's not really true, is it? Not yet.

"Grandma?"

There's no answer, of course. I shudder and draw away. I can't believe she's gone.

Last night before our gaming binge, I'd helped her with her wood, and after, had tea. Or at least, I'd had tea sweetened with honey and milk, and she'd opened a new bottle of champagne. Grandma didn't like to drink alone, so it was my nightly duty to be there.

On her TV table, a small glass jar held black fish eggs. She dipped her shaky pinky into it and sucked the eggs off before washing it down with the foam only half settled in her glass. Her trailer was behind my mom's. A silver bullet-shaped job, smaller, but you could tell it was nice when she first bought it. In front of the trailer were stacked three cords of uncut wood. That was what Grandma needed help with, not the champagne. She had trouble balancing the log that needed chopping atop the big, wide chopping stump, but she could still pop a cork.

I held the wood with my finger while Grandma peered down and squinted as though the whole scene swam. She hefted the axe and brought it down with enough force to bury the axe blade in the stump. If I timed it right, I'd release the log just as the axe struck. It wasn't so bad with the first couple of chops but with each cut, the piece I held shrank. And Grandma always took the same hard swing no matter how small the piece was that remained.

While she was swinging, she told me things I needed to do,

and the shining axe blade made it really difficult to say no. Once you're in a rhythm of saying yes, it's tough to keep concentrating on what someone's saying when that axe glints and arcs down toward your digits.

I try to remember now, because I'm fairly certain she'd said something like, "Yer seventeen now."

"Yes."

wince *Chop.*

"You don't know what life's about, RB."

"Yes, ma'am."

wince *Chop.*

"You're old enough to know it though."

"Yes."

WINCE *Chop.*

"Told the others the same thing at yer age."

"Yes."

"But none ever listened to me."

"Yes."

omg *Chop.*

"The meaning of life is as simple as . . ."

That's about when I faded out because to hold the little piece of kindling that remained, I had to rest my finger over top of where she'd hit. I wasn't thinking about the meaning of life, but deciding that my new nickname was about to become four-finger-Ray.

Blah, blah, blah. "You listening to me?"

"Yes."

Chop.

Two matchstick-thin pieces fell to either side of the stump. The axe handle quivered.

"And there you have it. That's the recipe for the meaning of life. What d'you know?" She looked at me with a rare smile. "One of yous listened. Maybe you will amount to something after all."

I may not know the meaning of life, but I have all my fingers. What *had* she said? What's the recipe for the meaning of life? I'd give my finger for it now.

I clench my eyes shut, but nothing comes to me. It doesn't seem fair. Poor Uncle Jamie—he deserves the park more than I do. He's her son! I never expected anything. Sure, my mom's mean, but it doesn't seem fair to her either.

In bed, I turn to Grandma. "Do you mind, Grandma, if I let the others have the park? Make them give me a few thousand dollars so I can pay first and last month's rent on a new place in town?"

It had been the cost of living keeping me here. It's hard to move out when you have no money to pay first and last. No job to sign a lease with. Not unless you want to move onto the streets, and then how would I start my gaming career? Until now, staying at the trailer park made sense. I have been slowly building a base of fans. One follower even "tips" me every so often with real money.

I swallow hard, panic building in my stomach. I don't have enough tips to pay rent.

I am in trouble. If I find the meaning of life, I'll own a trailer park my grandma wants me to keep running. That sure doesn't sound like the meaning of life to me. But if I give up without getting anything, then I have to move to town and get a dumb job and live who-knows-where.

I push myself onto my elbow. Grandma's mouth is open like she wants to say something, but her eyelids are down. "Not really fair, you know? Handing me the park after Mom's worked so hard for it. Said she'd pay for education, maybe. Maybe she'll put in a new playground or a big water slide. That would be fun, wouldn't it?"

I start thinking of sliding down a slide like that. And mini golf with one of those windmills you have to get the ball past; maybe Grandma's statue could be part of the course. She'd like that.

I sigh. It won't happen. My mom might sell the place, no matter what Grandma wanted. Besides, it's not that sort of trailer park.

The park's busy during most summers, but not with the folk you'd expect. Not families taking a break from the city heat. The only tourists who stay are lost, and they don't stay long.

Business is mostly from a group we call "jacks." It's the miners who come and work the mines north of here. Lumberjacks who cut timber. They dig or haul all day and come back to drink and burn something on their grills before heading back out the following shift. Jacks don't have much free time, and they don't worry about leaves in pools or mini golf.

Giving the park to Mom and Uncle Jamie is still the right thing to do, especially if it means I can move out and start gaming. Grandma just went a bit crazy at the end and changed her will. I swing my legs out of bed and pull on a sweatshirt, tucking my feet into boots. With the decision made, I head toward the fire to tell them, feeling better and smiling already at the thought of their reactions. A few grand ain't too much to ask.

And I start floating again, without the weight of needing to figure out the meaning of life, because it's heavier than it sounds.

Chapter 7

They've added wood to the fire. Everyone sits well back. Salminder has left for his trailer; he's tired a lot lately. The newlyweds are gone, too. Those who remain laugh so hard they don't hear me approaching.

"I'm gonna make a rocket!" Uncle Jamie says. "A rocket that everyone in a thousand miles will see when it bursts."

"Willing to guarantee that explosion at any rate," my mom says.

"I want an ATV, heated seats. And a new truck," Crystal says.

"Gonna sell this place and head to Las Vegas. Always say you need money to make money, and I'm gonna prove it," my mom replies.

"Where am I gonna go if you sell?" Uncle Jamie asks.

"A half a million dollars, Jamie, I don't care where you go! Or you could buy me out. Besides, where you getting the money for your rocket if you don't sell?"

"That's not what Ma wanted." Uncle Jamie frowns.

"Ma's dead, Jamie—we're not."

"I'm coming with you, though, right, Mama?" Crystal asks.

"Here's the way of things," Mom explains, going sober. "When my ma's dead, I get her stuff. When your ma's dead, you get my stuff. And I'm gonna win all sorts of stuff in Vegas, so yer the lucky one."

Crystal grins as if imagining all she's going to have decades from now.

It bugs me that Tina's still sitting with them. Every time I glance her way my chest hurts, and I imagine what it would be like to press my lips against hers.

"One more month," my mom says. "One more month, and then we're done. No more toilets to scrub. No more showers. No more trailers to clean and yahoos to keep quiet." She lifts her glass. Uncle Jamie tosses another one of his tiny bags onto the fire.

"Sounded like a fart, that one," Crystal says.

At the edge of the firelight, I hesitate. I remember the way my sister's rifle scope trained on me. *A rocket, gambling, a new truck.* They're deciding what to do with Grandma's money. The inheritance will go up in smoke in a few weeks. When Grandma comes back, she's coming back to nothing. But it's not my money, right? I don't *want* an RV park.

Maybe this is the push I need to leave here even sooner. I'm qualified to flip burgers. I can game nights and, when I'm making enough money at that, I can game full time. One day, I'll have a million fans and people will send me pizza whenever I say I'm hungry, just to keep me at the screen. There's gotta be places to flip burgers in town.

"How's about you don't need to wait a month?" I say. The only sound that comes after is the snap of sparks. I hustle into the quiet to sit on the log beside Tina. "What if I tell the lawyer I can't figure out the meaning of nothing and you get the park?"

Uncle Jamie tosses a packet into the embers and it farts pink.

"Pretty," Tina says. "How'd you make it burn pink?"

Uncle Jamie shrugs.

"Where's the hitch?" my mom asks me.

"No hitches," I say." I just want a few thousand dollars, enough to start in town."

"A few thousand dollars." My mom snorts. "You want money?"

"That's it." I smile, feeling better.

"Don't you understand, Ray?" Mom digs into her bra and holds up the will that says I get everything. "This says you get nothing."

I look to Uncle Jamie, but he doesn't meet my eye.

Crystal says, "No one knows the meaning of life. Old people die wondering, 'What the heck just happened?'"

"If you get everything but have to do something impossible to keep it, then that's just another way of saying nothing," Mom explains. "Unless you know the meaning of life, that is."

"Grandma told me, I only forgot," I say.

My mom bursts into laughter.

"People don't have crises when they're forty over nothing— no one's figured it out. And you sure won't be the first," Crystal says.

"You don't want the park?" I ask.

"Didn't say that," my mom replies, biting back her laughter. "But I can wait a month if it'll cost me money to get it. Do it for nothing, and you have a deal."

I stare at the pebbly eyes of my mother. They shine smiling-mean.

Crystal says, "I dunno, Ma, might be funny to watch him try."

Cold fear streaks through me. Clammy. Sweat. What're my options? Give them the park, and they'll just kick me off and I'll be on the street. If I stay, at least I have a month to save up the Pulled Beef tips I usually spend on new gaming gear. Tina gives me a look of wide-eyed pity.

"Maybe I'll—" Uncle Jamie starts, but shuts up under my mom's gaze.

"Don't you dare, Jamie," she says. "The boy needs to be taught a lesson."

Uncle Jamie offers an apologetic shrug.

"Okay, okay, maybe I will then," I reply. "Can't be so hard. There's the Internet and everything." It's just words, nothing important, right? But then why does my heart hammer?

I've never heard my mom giggle before, but she does now. "Can't be so hard?" she laughs. Tina reaches out slowly and covers my hand with hers. It's what I need to keep my chin up. Jamie pitches the rest of his sachets, and colors burst in the coals.

"Yes! Okay, Ray," my mom says through tears of mirth. It's a deal. An oath. "You can keep yer month and stay in that trailer, too." She checks her watch as if setting the timer.

"Meaning of life," Crystal says. "Hashtag Kraft Dinner."

And I know I'm in trouble.

Chapter 8

I wake face-to-face with Grandma, scream, fall out of bed, and then remember that I need to find the meaning of life. I clamber to my feet and hit the button on my computer. The screen stays dark. No power strip. I can't find the meaning of life with my computer down. And I'm not hungry enough to cook with a corpse in my trailer, so I skip breakfast.

It's still early as I leave the trailer and tug my gray hoodie over my ears. I tell myself to calm down. I've got a month. A whole month to get out of here. I sneak into one of the rental trailers, borrow an extension cord, and swap it for my power strip. Grandma's brain freezer bleeps at the interruption but restarts.

Back in my trailer, I swear only to game for ten minutes. Two hours later, I rub bleary eyes and hit search on Google. *What is the meaning of life?* After all, billions of people are on the Internet; surely someone knows. I might as well try the obvious.

On my screen, the first search hit is a video of three women dancing the hula. They're laden with flowers and waving their arms, smiling. Then a beaver chitters across the stage, once, twice, three times before bullets shower the scene and everyone's dead. It's all ketchupy. Over eighty-five million views.

In the comments is a message from someone calling themselves "Allofyou":

This video's right. There is no meaning. How can there be? When we die everything is forgotten. There is no purpose. And don't say 'going to heaven' because I don't believe in that.

The guy sounds like he'd be fun at parties. He does have a point though. Below another commenter disagrees: *So the meaning is legacy then. Being remembered.*

To which Allofyou replies: *A million years from now, no one will remember Bill Gates, or Steve Jobs, or Zuckerberg or Mother Theresa, let alone you. A million years is nothing in geologic time. All this save the Earth stuff, that's BS. It's about saving us. The Earth doesn't care, it'll be circling the sun a billion years from now and ants will rule the world.*

That seems to have shut the responder up. The Hawaiian Beaver Slaughter video is creeping over another million views, which may or may not disprove Allofyou's point. Eighty-five million views at one minute a pop is two eighty-year lifetime equivalents.

There's a knock at the door. Uncle Jamie.

"Wanted to say good morning to Ma," he says.

For a second I don't know what he means and then the air from outside hits me, the pine and crisp freshness of late spring, and it's sweet. The door slams shut and the air in here turns not-so-sweet once more.

Uncle Jamie steps into the trailer. Grandma's arms lowered over the course of the night, and she no longer looks as though she's ready to pop out of bed. But the rest of her hasn't improved any.

"Uncle, what's the meaning of life?"

He pauses. "This about the will?"

"Well, yes, mostly. It is, but . . . why am I here?"

"I can answer that one. Your mom went and met a man who—"

"That's not what I meant," I say. "What do you think the meaning of life is?"

"Honestly?" Uncle Jamie sags a bit. "To not leave much of a mark. I mean there's only so much of everything. Who am I to take it?"

"So, no meaning." His response is actually sadder than that. It's like he feels he's a tax on the planet and it would be better off without him. "Why the fireworks then? They're not really good for the environment or anything."

He flushes and waves me off. "Need a job, don' I?"

I've never seen him sell any of his fireworks. There's more to it than that. "You could do a different job."

"Closest thing I can get to magic . . ." He's gone totally red. "Don't want another job because this one's the closest thing I can get to magic."

I'm about to ask him what he means, but his eyes have settled on Grandma. He's not ready to let her go.

Back at the screen I read a few quotes. Arnold Schwarzenegger says the meaning of life's *to move ahead, to achieve, to go up. To conquer.* Uh, conquer what? Life?

The meaning of life is to give life meaning. What the . . . ?

These people are crazy; why do I even bother? Crystal was right. After surfing some jobs in town, I bring up the game, *Arcane Dynasty*, and start casting fireballs at dragon hybrids. My speakers blare with lightning bolts and clashing swords. Uncle Jamie shouts for me to shut it down. I mute the volume and then fumble for my headset. Dragon spawn are everywhere, and I'd forgotten how far I'd gotten before succumbing last time.

I'm playing for Grandma. This morning I will level up.

Plugged in, I don't even notice my uncle leave, but the sweet outdoors washes over me before I'm back in rank dead Grandma and congealing Kraft Dinner stink.

Chapter 9

I'm opening the pool because that's probably the meaning of life. Next I'll flip meaningful burgers. Today's a big day for the park—you could say it's *its* meaning of life. The first official day that we're open for the summer. Crystal's burnishing toilet seats. I don't want my mom bugging me about smoothing the road ruts, which has to be one of the worst jobs ever now that Grandma doesn't need me to hold her wood. Road ruts and the pool, those were the chores I said I'd keep doing for as long as I stuck around. Crystal and Mom do everything else: all the bills, reservations, cleaning trailers, emptying trash, washrooms, showers, and, with Grandma dead, they'll have to cut the wood too.

Despite the importance of the day and the pickups with trailers winding their way up Sunny Days' drive, my mom's spending the morning clearing out Grandma's trailer with Uncle Jamie. I hear her crying sometimes, and I wonder how that's possible. For the last three years she's only scowled at me. Never even reminded me to eat my fruits and vegetables. I only started eating lettuce and tomatoes on burgers after Doc diagnosed my bleeding gums as a vitamin deficiency. *Who gets scurvy?*

As I skim leaves off the top of the rubber pool cover, Deneze—pronounced Den-knee-ze, one of the guys from the garbage truck—comes up to the pool fence.

"Sorry about the old lady, huh," Deneze says. "Wanted to stop by to see everyone's okay." A shock of black hair hangs down his back, his face stoic with pronounced smile lines despite his being only a few years older than me.

"Thanks, Deneze, wasn't your fault. Bear got her."

"Weird, huh? Bears are known in my tribe to have powerful wisdom. Sometimes we consider them elders."

I pause mid-skim. My grandma wouldn't be happy to know she was killed by a reborn First Nations elder from the neighboring reservation. But maybe there was a reason for it all. I mean, if I believe we have a purpose, then maybe the whole fireball/squirrel/dream catcher/bear thing had meaning too. "What's the meaning of life for you?" I ask.

He bursts out laughing. "Garbage collecting, obviously."

"Seriously." I pause.

Both of us stop to listen to the honks of irritated drivers trying to reverse into tight slabs.

"I don't know," Deneze replies, "but if I ask an elder they'll probably send me on a vision quest." He's laughing again, but he didn't answer my question, and I have only twenty-nine days.

"A vision quest's a bad thing? I've heard about them on, you know, on television and in books. But how do I take a vision quest?"

For a moment he hesitates, as if caught out. Even looks angry for a second, but I've known Deneze ever since his father started letting him ride the backs of the trucks a decade ago. "I dunno actually, I never did one, but my dad did. Said he went into the woods and lived there until he had a vision and the vision gave him his totem and what he was supposed to do."

"Whoa." That sounds pretty easy actually. "So what did he do?"

Deneze shrugs. "Started a paving company."

It seems weird that an owl or coyote or something would appear to a human and suggest that what they really need are more roads and parking lots; still, a vision quest seems better than what I found on the Internet.

"Can I go on a vision quest?" I ask.

"Don't white people have their own version?" he snaps.

"Sorry. I know it's kinda racist, assuming First Nations to be mystical and all, but you do seem more . . . I don't know. White people have to wait until half their life's gone before they sort it out."

Deneze shrugs. "Okay, well, anyone can go on a vision quest, but there's a lot of preparation."

"I was thinking about climbing the Big this summer. How does your quest work?"

"Well, first you have to fast for four days." A dragonfly hovers over the pool and draws Deneze's gaze.

"Fast, like not eat much?" Half my attention's on the pool and avoiding the block of ice filling it, the other half on the conversation.

"Fast—meaning don't eat at all. Nothing but a little water."

I dump a scoop of leaves on the poolside. "For four days? You guys are crazy."

"And climbing a mountain's smarter? At least I know how to not eat."

"I can climb. I've been watching YouTube videos."

Deneze laughs. "What's the meaning of life for white people then?"

I shake my head. It's actually pretty obvious what most people think. "Make lots of money. Get famous." That's pretty much my plan, isn't it? To become a gamer extraordinaire.

"My father's the richest in the tribe, owns the garbage company now, too." This seems to sadden him for some reason. "He nailed it."

"So you're set then," I say.

He flushes crimson. "So are you, I hear—old lady left you everything."

"Yeah, just need to tell the lawyer the meaning of life."

"Oh."

We both fall silent, watching the dragonfly hover amid the bangs and shouts of opening day.

"Don't think 'make lots of money' will be the answer, do you?" Deneze asks.

"Nope." I sigh because deep down something tells me gaming isn't going to be it, either. I go back to skimming, shooing the dragonfly over the fence and back into the forest.

"Let me know when you have the answer," Deneze says. "Maybe the mountain will share it. But no one can take a pee for you." The son of the richest man in the area disappears back toward a gate plugged with RVs. After a minute his ATV rumbles to life.

I scrape at leaves half-stuck in the ice and know I'll never get them all . . . and that the ice will just melt and scatter more leaves into the pool.

The whole thing seems so pointless.

Chapter 10

Maybe Tina or Salminder know the meaning of life. Salminder's really religious—he'll have stuff figured out. I'd gone looking for him earlier, but no one answered when I knocked on his trailer.

Campfire smoke infuses the air as campers settle into their new homes for the next couple months. As if on cue, mosquitoes have descended. It's like they were breeding their army, like Sauron his legions of orcs, off in the oily swamp that runs from the edge of camp to beneath Big Mountain. In its stagnant waters, the mosquitoes congregated, sharing food, sharpening their needle mouths, teaching the youngsters swarming techniques, where the sweetest blood is and the myth of how, every year at this time, a feast is prepared for them at Sunny Days RV Park—their meaning of life—swarm on!

Thoughts like this might be why I don't have a girlfriend.

So far this spring, the black flies had been a typical nuisance, but I've never seen this many mosquitoes. Their high-pitched whines are steady. I pass campers decked out in full netting, others bathing in Muskol, and the rest flailing at the near-invisible insects bent on achieving their destinies.

After seventeen springs here, I still hate the mosquitoes just as much and smack and swipe at my arms and neck in a near continuous frenzy as I jog toward Pulled Beef to take my shift. The line's already across the patio stones, tables filled with a dozen campers who bury their faces in burger buns. Tina beams at a new customer as I arrive, arms windmilling and spackled with tiny bloody carcasses.

Tina laughs at me. "You started searching for your Zen yet?"

"Zen's not the same as meaning," I reply.

Opening weekend's tough at the grill. Most campers rush to claim the best berths before doing their grocery shopping. It'll be nonstop all day at Pulled Beef. On the plus side, with the grill going full fry, the mosquitoes keep back, even with the hole in the trailer. I quicken my pace across the patio, and the pursuing mosquito horde scatters to mow down on the waiting campers.

"Where's Salminder?" I ask, breathing heavily and cocking my ear for the telltale approach of the enemy bugs.

"Nice to see you, too. You're late."

"Am not," I retort. "Not as late as usual, anyway. That's saying something because this morning I reached the next level in *Arcane Dynasty*. I'm officially a Mage."

"My dad's in town getting more patties before it gets busy." Another three people join the line as we talk. A weight pulls at my shoulders; I'd hoped Salminder could help. He's the father I never even knew, doubt my mother even knew, and has been at the camp for who knows how long. He drove me to the hospital in town when I broke my arm. He convinced me to stay in school when I wanted to drop out last year—jury's out on if that was the right call. I have one year left, and the only thing holding me there now is Salminder's suggestion that I keep my options open.

If I'm kicked out of camp, I know what I'll need to do: make money to eat.

On the grill, flames lick the edges of twelve patties at various stages of being turned into the consistency of shoe leather. I pick up the spatula and start flipping, sending columns of flame toward the ceiling. In a small space at the corner of the grill, I make up Ray's special sauce—a mess of mustard, onions, ketchup, relish, garlic, mayo, and hot sauce, all fried to a thick goo.

Tina cringes from it. "Just don't serve that to an actual customer by mistake."

I lean over the grill and let the grease and scents infuse me. There's a Zen to burger flipping. For one thing, no matter how large the line is, I can only cook twelve burgers at a time. It took me two summers to stop fretting about the line and to focus on the cooking. Under food safety laws, I must cook the meat until the patties could be used as lethal weapons if thrown hard enough. In other words, I can't rush the burger. For another thing, the flames are mesmerizing. Maybe this is why Uncle Jamie likes fireworks too.

The business of dealing with customers fades to the background as I flip, flip, flip, flip. And then thunk, four ready patties into the steel dish.

Done, done, done, done.

The grill's the bottleneck. Tina's fast. At the condiments command center she deals out cheese, pickles, onions—*I said hold the onions!*—mustard, relish, and ketchup.

Sometimes if I'm lucky she'll sing a little. Never a pop tune, always something I've never heard, and I'd swear it's timed to the rhythm of the flash and sizzle of me at the grill. We're in sync. Today she's quiet and somehow darkened. Normally, she'd be excited about the start of a new summer, talking about school and everything that's happened since. That's okay because I have lots to think about.

Tina and I work as a team, but it's the first day, and I'm rusty, missing, scraping, burning, swearing. It's been an hour at the grill already and if anything the line's longer, when this guy asks for "Swami Raymond."

"You mean Ray?" Tina asks and looks back at me, where I shake my head.

"Swami, wah?" I wipe my hands on my apron and turn the grill down before approaching the counter. "I'm Ray," I say, leaning out. The day's warmed, but the air's still cooler than the inside of the fry-truck.

"Okay, Swami Ray then, what's my fortune?" About two-thirds of the campers look like jacks. Bearded, denim-wearing, plaid-jacketed. Half of these are miners, half cut trees. I can usually tell the difference because of the sawdust in their beards or the oily shine of their foreheads, but no one's had their first shifts yet. This guy is one of those types. He slides a five-dollar bill onto the counter.

"What are you talking about?" I ask.

He hands me a coupon that's been run through the office photocopier. I can tell because Crystal scratched a penis into the glass of the photocopier when she was a teen, and now every copy that comes out of the office has a penis. All the handouts have it. Fun at the Campfire—penis. Camp Amenities, pool, play park—penis. I wonder if I would have gotten along better with teenager-Crystal than I do with twenty-five-year-old Crystal.

The coupon has a black border, and written in thick black type is: "This entitles the bearer to one fortune telling by Swami Raymond the Magnificent, Knower of the Meaning of Life.* With purchase of burger"—penis.

"The girl at the office gave it to me, said it comes with the site."

Tina sniggers. "Crystal—okay, that's a pretty good one. Have a bite, learn the meaning of life. We should be charging more."

At least three others in line are holding the same coupon I hand back to the guy.

There's something about the desperate sheen to his eyes though. Every other part of him looks bagged. The swathes beneath his eyes. The bloodless lips and blotchy skin above his furry cheeks. His plaid sweater-coat has patches and the hems of his jeans are frayed. But his eyes sparkle with expectation.

"Sorry, I don't tell fortunes. That's just my sister making fun. What do you want on your burger?"

His gaze saddens before dipping down to the coupon. The fiver disappears back into his jean's pocket, and he starts to leave. He wanted the future more than the burger? It's stupid but shame fills me, disappointment in my disappointing the guy.

"Come on, Ray," Tina whisper-urges.

The light's back in her eyes, the smile full again, so I know I have to try. I scour my mind for something pithy. "It'll be fine, you know," I say. He glances back over his shoulder. "Life— today at least," I hedge. "It'll be a good one. A bit noisy tonight and be sure to get up early for the showers. Hot water runs out." Are camping tips the same as fortunes? "If the bear's brown lay down, if it's black fight back. Oh, and wear light-colored clothing to keep mosquitoes away." Half the jacks in line groan.

The fortune seeker doesn't come back to buy a burger, but his chin lifts as he moves away. I return to the grill, trying to find that elusive Zen.

Flip, flip, flip, flip.

Done, done, done, done.

Chapter 11

After standing over the grill for seven hours, I step out of the trailer with oil dripping from my chin. In one hand is a Ray Special and in the other are the crumpled fortune coupons of some dozen disappointed customers. They all got the same one from me—*things'll be fine*. But they won't, will they? Of the twelve, someone will get cancer, a couple will have heart attacks. Maybe one will become mixed up in drugs or alcohol. Not a one will strike it rich, half will get married and have kids. And then die. I want to read the rest of the will, to figure out if those double asterisks are important. I still don't trust my mother's, "Oh, that's nothing."

Customers who arrived later got better fortunes from Salminder. He shouted from where he stocked the freezer: "Can't have rainbows without rain." Or, "Success has no elevator—take the stairs." But he didn't stay long, saying he saw a nap in his future.

I go to slick my hair back, my fingers catching the hairnet and pulling it off. I drop the coupons in the overflowing trash, pause, knowing I should help Salminder by emptying the garbage. But I hear another request for Swami Raymond and so hurry away toward my mom's trailer before Tina can call me back.

Instead I hear her shout, "Great things always seem impossible until they are done." I grin because I feel as though she's talking to me.

The camp's transformed since morning. I like this time of year. Not the mud, or the bugs, but the influx of fresh blood. Or maybe's it's just Tina occupying more of my thoughts than normal. I can still feel the heat of her hand over mine from the campfire.

If two-thirds of campers are lonely jacks of the miner or lumberjack kind, there are a few who are joined by their spouses and, once in a while, a screaming kid. These rare families are tired, tired, and they are the most demanding campers because someone's at the trailer all day, and camp's boring, the swimming pool isn't open, the playground is a hundred years old, and the only games you can play on the rusted structure are, "Get tetanus. Loose a limb. Crack your chin." It should be condemned, but that would mean losing a key selling feature for the trailer park.

The rest of the campers are like a box of assorted chocolates: An old retiree who's run out of savings and is headed back here for seasonal work. A few outsiders who just aren't good with people, real loners dressed in black and camouflage, survivalists fading as much as possible into the landscape. I spot a family that mistakenly thought this was good place to "get in touch with nature," and finally an immensely fat man who's saying to a jack that every year the camp hosts a great monster truck rally— which isn't at all true.

A web of wash lines is strung between trees with some Christmas lights. Patio furniture is laid out. A few campers put up signs: *Welcome to the Jones'. This is how we roll. Home is where we park it.* The scents of cooking meat, popcorn, bug spray, and stale campers permeate the air. The sun dips to the treetops, but every day we get a few more minutes of light. This far north, it's nearly midnight before full dark at the solstice.

Tires have turned the road into an even soupier mess. I know full well what my mom will ask me to do this evening. I listen at the office door to make sure she's not around and hear my sister on the phone. I plan to snoop around and search for the will.

Even so, I rap twice. The office doubles as my mom and sister's trailer, and Lord knows I don't want to catch them naked or anything, so knocking's a good idea.

"It's open," Crystal calls, and I haul open the door. "Oh, it's you. What's the meaning of life, Swami Raymond?" Her lips clench, and I can tell she's barely holding back her mirth.

I crumple the coupons stacked on the kitchen table, which is also covered in paperwork.

Crystal bursts into laughter.

"It's bothering Salminder," I lie. "Slows down the line." That part's true.

"You only have one thing on the menu," she says. "Who cares?"

"Pool still isn't open," my mom adds, stepping out of the washroom. She's rubbing her towel at her hair and totally nude. Everything jiggles. I twist away.

"Aw, Mom," I say and claw at my eyes as if I can rid them of the memory. My heart sinks. She won't *hand* me the will, not without a fight.

"You can turn back now, I'm covered. When you opening that pool?"

I crack an eyelid. She has a towel wrapped around her. It's not enough. "Has an iceberg floating in it still," I say. "Where's the will?"

"Why?" she asks and glances back toward her bedroom. Their trailer is much larger than mine and has two bedrooms, a washroom, kitchen, and living area. The whole place smells of potpourri and doesn't rock with every movement. Above the floral curtains hang my sister's rifles. On the opposite wall a crossbow.

"There was another asterisk, two of them. A footnote or something that I never read," I say.

She shifts uncomfortably. "I'll get it to you later, if I finds it."

"Finds it? What'd you do with it? Burn it too?"

Her face keeps twitching, but I'd caught that look back to her bedroom. "Yeah, I burned it. I did it. Was mad, see."

I pause, wondering if I should call her bluff. I could hitch a ride into town to find Sam Peregrine, but I won't have a chance for a few days. Or I can sneak in here and take it back. It's mine anyway. No need to tip her off that I know she's lying though. "You remember what it said?" I ask.

She shakes her head. I know it's a lie again because she's never quiet about anything.

"I need you to smooth that road tonight or it'll be concrete when the rain stops. Road grader costs money."

"Crystal can," I say. In *Arcane Dynasty*, the rest of my party, which includes people from all over the real world, are waiting to take on our first dragon. I might even save my first princess.

They'll do it all without me if I don't get back to my screen soon.

"Crystal is helping settle the campers and cleaning bathrooms."

"The ruts just keep coming back anyways," I say.

Her fists find her hips. "So does mold and dirt and grime," she says. "And what's supposed to happen when you figure out the meaning of life? You going to let the washrooms go? Stop paying Deneze?"

"You can stay and help," I say, and her eyes narrow. "Fine, I'll just sell it then."

My mom's lips stretch into a pencil-thin line. Then comes this smile that scares me. She begins stabbing a finger toward me. "Crystal, how'd you like a vacation?" she asks.

Crystal looks up from where she's frowning at bills. "Like to a beach?"

"No, a staycation," Mom says. "The entertainment will be right here."

"What're you talking about, Mom?" I ask, but I already know that I don't want an answer.

"I won't need to scrub none of the toilets?" Crystal asks suspiciously. "No toothbrush on the shower mold? Or scraping that stuff I-never-know-what-it-is that hangs from the ceiling?"

"None of that," my mom replies.

"Who's gonna do it?" Crystal scratches at her bleached hair.

I know what my mom's thinking, but I don't know why she thinks it's right.

"You're mulling the meaning of things, right, son?" she asks, still stabbing her index finger at me. I nod. "So that you can win the trailer park."

"It's not winning, Mom, it's what Grandma wanted and I would've given you—"

She holds up her palm. "So why am I busting my butt for your park?"

"It's not my park yet."

"It's not mine either. It's like Schrödinger's cat."

"What?"

"I dunno. I only know I'm not taking care of something you could own. And you gotta run it until you lose, or you give up."

I stand there dumbfounded, and finally Crystal gets the joke or at least realizes enough of it that she leaps up from the chair and starts jumping up and down.

She whoops.

"Get out the lounge chairs, Crystal, this is gonna be something to watch."

"Who is going to run the park?" I ask. "Who is going to do everything?"

"Here's the keys, son," she says.

She tosses an imaginary set that I go to catch like an idiot.

"I won't be paying you then," I say. "You won't have anything to live on."

But she's ahead of me because she's still smiling.

"I have enough squirreled away, Ray, and none of that will matter in a month. After that I'll be rich."

"I'll just walk away then, if you don't want to stay. I'm just selling the land anyways."

That smile's stuck on her face, and I so want to peel it off.

"Don't know how you'll feed yourself then," she says. "Can't sell the park until you know the meaning of life."

"What do you mean? Salminder pays me."

"And if you walk away how's Salminder going to make money? Hmm? Or Tina?"

I don't know what she sees in my face at the mention of Tina, but both she and Crystal giggle.

"I'll have time to go back after that bear, Mama! I knows it's out there watching and waiting, just like it did for Grandma." Crystal grins.

"How's Jamie going to eat? He's got nothing," my mom adds. "If you don' like it, give me the keys and forget about ever finding the meaning of life."

I clutch the imaginary keys, wanting to throw them back. "But—"

She has me. I own the park until I can't tell the lawyer the meaning of life, then I can finally let it go again. I could forfeit. Let it go right now and not look back, but then they'll have won, and I'll be out, homeless, penniless, and directionless. The reality is, I can't let Tina down.

I shove the keys into my pocket. My boots have never felt so heavy as I slog out of the trailer and into the muddy mess of the trailer park. My trailer park. I step into a tire track, the sheer sides up to my knees. On the road ahead a pickup spins its wheels, spewing blue exhaust and spraying mud. I'm gonna hate this time of year.

I grab a shovel from the equipment shed and start filling ruts.

Chapter 12

I wake to banging.

It's dark. It smells . . . better.

I flip onto my side. Grandma's gone.

My first thought is: Grandma's now a zombie or a vampire, risen from the dead, and storming the camp. A were-bear? No, it's not a full moon. Zombie then, since she's missing her brain. But that's ridiculous, because why would she have left without eating *my* brain first?

Bang, bang, bang.

"Hey!" A voice like oil sands.

I switch on my light. Still looking for Grandma. How did I not hear someone sneak in and steal her? And why would anyone do that?

BANG, BANG!

Sporting only my undies, I open the door.

A man stands there, blinking. Bugs cloud the yellow porch light.

"No hot water," the man says.

"Go talk to the office," I mumble and shut the door.

BANG, BANG—

Halfway to the bed, I stumble back to the door.

The man's brow's furrowed, and he points to the side of my trailer. I lean out. Someone's spray-painted OFFICE in big black letters.

"What time is it?" I ask.

"Four. First shift at the mine's at five."

"Well . . ." I think hard for a way to get back to bed. "We don't have hot water here."

"What're you talking about?" The voice rises.

"Yeah, this here's an eco-friendly camp," I say.

"Eco?"

"Yeah, environmentally friendly. Heating the water takes energy. And we don't believe in wasting all that fuel. Warming the Earth and killing everyone. Do you want to kill everyone?"

"I jes' want a shower's all." He looks chastened for a second and then glances back up. "You know that everyone here either mines oil all day or chops down trees?" I swallow as the man's face reddens, and then comes his tentative smile. "Wait a second, you're joshing with me."

I'm not. I really, really want to go back to sleep, but the glow of another flashlight sways up the trail.

"Yeah, joshing." I pull on pants and a hoodie and then lead the growing number of annoyed campers back toward the showers. "I can try to fix it, but the water's not gonna be hot for a while."

Their faces droop with the realization that I'm right and no amount of complaining will help reheat the hot water tank. At the back of the shower building hunkers a concrete block shed that holds the tank and cleaning supplies. I go inside and plug the propane ignition button a few times to ignite the pilot. Never goes out like this, so I don't know what happened. Anyway, I stomp back toward bed, while campers grumble inside and gasp under cold spray. A pickup truck starts and someone shouts for quiet, but it's too late for that. I pause at the entry to the path to my trailer. A picket sign points out: *Office.*

I pick up the shovel I dropped last night and go to take a swing at the sign before realizing that it's only going to lead to people wandering around looking for who's in charge and being even more angry when they finally find me.

I hang my head. I could just leave, hitchhike into town, sleep on a bench somewhere, find work where I can. But then what about Tina? What about the princesses that need rescuing and the dragons that need slaying in *Arcane Dynasty*? My fans? I shake my head. I'll give it the month. Twenty-eight days.

I turn back to where I stopped filling ruts last night and start digging. Sun will be up in an hour.

***

"I need my cash," Uncle Jamie says.

I shake awake. I fell asleep leaning on the shovel. Sun's up. I vaguely recall someone taking a selfie with me, but other than that I don't remember much.

"Crystal says you have the cash now," he says.

"What? I don't have anything. Stop believing Crystal. And why does my mom give you cash anyways?"

He flushes. "Always does, every month, five hundred for expenses."

"Expenses."

"Fireworks."

"You said you sell them."

"I will. Still working on the right recipe."

"Right, well, I have to get money from my mom. She gave me the imaginary keys but no actual cash."

Uncle Jamie shakes his head as I go to bang on her trailer.

"Why you bothering the tenants?" Crystal squints at me through a mud mask.

"You're not a tenant," I say. "I thought camo-paint was your beauty regime."

She squints and the mask cracks. "We don't work here no more, but we live here. So we're tenants." She starts to pull the door shut but I catch it with my boot.

"I need the money," I say. "How am I supposed to run the park without money?"

"Go make some. Oh, right, you're not used to having to do stuff yourself, are you?"

"Where's Mom?" I demand. Crystal's hauling on the door and kicking at my toe. "Mom!" Mom stumbles out of her room buck naked and giggles. "Aw, stop doing that." I slap my palms across my eyes. "I need the checkbook."

My sister stops fighting, turns away and pushes past my mother to go to the washroom. They have hot water.

"I got a towel wrapped." My mom scratches at the fuzz growing on her chin. "Bank will need to change everything, not worth doing for a month," she says. "How's this? I'll sign the checks for you."

"Fine. Jamie says you give him money."

She shakes her head. "Nope. He always asks though. Let him steal the food he needs." She shuts the door on me.

"I'm filing a complaint with management." The door muffles Crystal's voice, but their laughter's loud and clear. I slump into one of the lawn chair's sagging webbing.

"You the manager?" It's a young woman with a little girl in pigtails. The girl's wearing a swimsuit, and the mom has towels over her shoulder.

I sigh. "Yes."

"I'm going swimming!" the girl exclaims.

"When will the pool be open?" the mother demands.

"Soon," I say. "Soon."

The trailer door reopens and out topples a mop, a bundle of rags, and pails.

"Toilet's plugged," someone shouts from the washroom.

"Plunger's in the shed with the rest," my mom hollers from the trailer. Crystal bursts back into laughter. I've never heard them laugh so much.

The mother of the girl purses her lips as I gather up a couple pails filled with gear and shuffle off, the handles biting into the pads of my fingers.

Chapter 13

Plunge the toilet.

Clean the toilets. Someone vomited on the floor.

Scrub the showers.

Repair the water line. *Duct tape!*

Fill the ruts.

Chip at pool berg.

Late for lunch shift—flip a couple hundred burgers while arguing with Tina about how I'm *never* on time. I don't remember fighting with her so much. Every time I talk to her she either tears up or grits her jaw like she's ready to deliver a right hook. I wish I could tell her that she's half the reason I'm still here, but that's a bit too much honesty.

Clean the rental trailers.

Take reservations.

Calm the wannabe nature-loving family.

Give non-nature-loving family money back.

Chop wood for campfire.

Return phone call from propane guy, the garbage company, and the funeral parlor . . . this one's worth elaborating on. I'd forgotten about Grandma's early morning departure, and it suddenly seemed obvious to me how it had happened. If not resurrection, or a zombie apocalypse, there really could only be one alternative.

"We'll be by to pick up your grandma around four," the cool voice says. "I'm so sorry for your loss. She was a delight. A lovely lady. A pillar of decency."

Everything's such a blur that I almost agree without thinking and then stop. "You already have her," I say.

There's a pause. "I'm sorry, sir, but we don't."

"Yes, you do." There really are no other options—the funeral parlor must have arrived in the dead of night and collected her body.

"Nope."

"If you don't have Grandma, then where is she?"

I'm sitting in Mom's trailer since it has the only landline. I can hear my mom outside telling people the manager will be right out.

"Would you like to cancel the appointment?" The voice on the phone cools further.

I can't imagine how she's looking round about now. I sense her statue staring. Her brain's still there—I checked on the green bars.

"Hold on," I tell the funeral man, jog to the door, and shove it open. "Where's Grandma?"

My mom looks at me. "Yer the one sleeping with her."

The big bear of a lumberjack man waiting for the manager covers his mouth.

"Isn't like that," I tell him. "She's dead."

He gags a little.

"I mean we just slept together is all, with her dead . . . aww, forget it."

The man must no longer need to talk, because he runs off toward the washroom.

"Grandma wasn't in my bed this morning," I say. "She's missing."

"Not like she wandered off," my mom scoffs.

"I have to go flip burgers," I say.

"Sites twenty-nine, eight, and sixty-five all want to see you," she says. "Don't know where that jack was from."

"Can't you—" I begin, but she's put on sunglasses and lies back down in the chair beside Crystal, who snores.

"If I have to keep taking messages like this, you're gonna have to start paying me," my mom says.

I cancel the hearse and head off toward Pulled Beef. Sites eight and sixty-five are on the way.

At site eight, the pigtailed girl asks about the pool again.

"There's a big block of ice in it," I say. She just blinks. "The ice is full of leaves, and I have to wait for it to melt in order to clean the pool."

"Tomorrow?" she squeaks, eyes shining with tears.

"Yeah, maybe tomorrow," I say.

The mother squints at me. "She was excited about the camp having a pool."

Stupid leaving the water in the pool all winter. Of course, that was me, but it was my mom's camp. At that point anyway. She could have pumped it out.

Site sixty-five has the rather plump man.

"Camp life starts early round here," he grumbles. His blue-and-white striped PJ pants are pulled up to his hairy chest, so he looks a lot like the Gaul Obelix in the *Asterix* comics. Funny, the mosquitoes buzz in a blurry halo around him but don't bite despite what must be a rather tempting canvas. His tiny Jack Russell barks up at me. "What's this I hear about no truck rally?"

"Sorry, sir, but we've never held a truck rally."

He tries a different tact. "You have enough mud for one."

That is true, but not for long. The ruts are as big as ever and the sun high. They're hardening. I'll need to spend the night working on them or else call in a road grader.

"Sorry," I repeat and then rush over to where Tina's poking her head out of Pulled Beef's window. "Sorry," I tell her.

Even though Tina and I have been arguing as of late, it's a relief to be here. This is where I've spent the last three summers; this is normal, a refuge. Last shift had been so awkward, without our usual banter. I'm relieved when I sense a bit of the old Tina back.

"So happy you're here," she says. "Salminder's in town getting more lettuce or something."

Tina has all the condiments and toppings out already. The salad bin is full. "Maybe he's expecting a run on extra lettuce?" I suggest. "For all the vegetarian jacks?" I can count them on one hand.

Tina bites her lip. "Yeah, maybe. Come on, get cooking. I need your help before the rush."

"And here I thought you were just interested in me for all of my money."

She laughs and my heart lifts. "You don't have any money."

"So if I did, you'd be interested?"

"No," she says in a don't-be-ridiculous tone.

I pause. "Why not?" I ask, beginning to scrape down the grill.

"You're such a dork." Her laughter isn't mean even though it cuts. It's lilting, like how a butterfly flies.

"What do you mean?" I ask. "A dork?"

Tina's smile fades and she looks away. "I didn't mean . . . *dork-dork*."

I step away from the grill to stand in front of her, unable to let it go.

"It's just been busy." She starts chopping tomatoes.

Dismayed that the awkwardness is back, I let the silence stretch.

Chop, choppity, chop.

"Okay I did mean it, but not in a really bad way," she says. "You live in a trailer."

"So do you," I reply, and return to scraping the scabs of grease.

"No, I sleep in a trailer during the summer. You *live* there. Choose to live there. You play video games every night. Used to be all day, too. At school you don't do anything, you let other people in your work groups do all of it. You're smart, but you're lazy. You don't try."

I toss the brush I'm using. It clangs against the iron grill. I don't feel lazy anymore. Not after today. I feel as though I've made up for a full year's laziness in a single day, so I bristle. "And what are you doing that's so special?" I demand.

"I'm trying." She nicks herself and sucks on her finger. Are those tears in her eyes? My heart goes out to her, but my brain's still angry.

"Trying what?" I ask.

"I want to learn things. I don't want to work at Pulled Beef." Her finger's bleeding still, but I'm not letting her off the hook. I've been taking it from campers, my mom, from Crystal, even Jamie, who keeps stealing the firewood I cut for the evening fire. What Tina said about school may be true, but if she had to hitchhike to and from school most of the time, and miss half the winter for snow, maybe she wouldn't be the star pupil either.

"Sorry, I didn't quite hear that," I say.

"I don't want to spend my life in Pulled Beef." She lowers her voice as if worried her father will hear.

"What do you want to do?" I ask.

"I dunno, okay, just not do this for any longer than I need to. Do I have to know everything?" There are tears on her cheeks now and I back off. She's never said anything mean to me before. I don't understand it, but I let it go.

"I do," I mumble. "I have to know." I have twenty-eight days to know everything. I yank open the freezer door to grab a box of hamburger patties.

"It's just money."

"Just a MILLION dollars," I say, standing in a fog of frosted air.

"Okay, maybe you would be a bit more interesting with a million dollars," she admits.

I smile. The will, the responsibility of the park, or maybe the pressure of the meaning of life, it's this chunk of ice floating in my stomach. For a moment, looking at her downward sloping eyes, I can forget about it. I can recall the press of her hand on mine, even if I know now it was only out of pity.

With the meat pucks on the counter I snatch the first-aid kit and peel open a bandage with a cartoon print. "Raymond Saintbury, lazy, dork . . . millionaire, knower of the meaning of life," I say. "Quite the catch."

"You any closer to figuring it out?" she asks, offering her slender brown finger, blood sliding to the tip. I glance up, expecting to see her joking, but her dark eyes are steady. There's the ice again.

"Somehow, I'm actually farther away." I grip her finger and press the cut into the bandage before securing the adhesive. We hold for a moment longer than strictly necessary before I let go. We lapse back to silence. Maybe that's safer.

As I fill ruts that evening, the same ruts I filled the evening before, I can see how it happens, how people stop searching for meaning. Everyone has these ruts to fill. If they don't fill them, they turn to concrete and can never be filled, so they keep at it every day. That's the real rut.

Chapter 14

The double asterisks have become a symbol of hope. Maybe desperation. It's not surprising. The first asterisk saved me from being mistaken for a bear. For an entire week, I do nothing but run, clean, dig, flip. I even take an axe to the pool-berg, but it's still too big and that's only the one on top of the cover. I've discovered an even bigger one beneath. The double asterisks hold all the answers.

After the first few days I gave up asking my mom for the will. So I called Sam Peregrine, but she never seemed to be in and if she returned my calls, then no one's giving me the messages. Crystal's probably just grumpy because she hasn't bagged her bear yet, likely because it's smarter than she is. But I don't have time to hang around the office and wait for Sam Peregrine's call.

I even tried to hitch a ride into town one morning, but Tina caught me at the gate and tapped her watch, reminding me about my shift. Finally I email Sam Peregrine and get an out-of-the-office reply. She'll be back in two weeks—a week and a half, now. There's nothing I can do but hold on like the kitten in one of those motivational posters—*Hang in there*.

Every day I lose a bit more sleep, and every day I get a little closer to begging my mom to take over and to forget the whole million-dollar thing.

With three weeks to go, she still laughs as I pass her. Sometimes the glee sounds forced, though. It's getting old for both of us. Once, I even catch her wiping down the counters in the women's washroom as if she can't help herself. Crystal's gone off hunting again. At least someone has what they want.

There's a routine to the chores, sure, but it's a grinding routine, one that stretches me a bit more every day and will eventually pull too far and leave me dislocated and limp. I have begun avoiding the little pigtailed girl and almost snapped at her the last time she asked about the pool. The ice in my guts has swollen. I'm not even hungry anymore.

Still don't know where Grandma went. I asked Uncle Jamie, but he only shrugged and kept stealing wood. For what, I don't know. There's a near continuous trail of white smoke about a half a mile into the woods. I'm suspicious he's working on his biggest fireworks yet. Something too big to be safely made in camp. His *rocket*. I was only eight at the time, but I still remember the summer when the whole trailer park was nearly flattened by one of his experiments.

The only thing I know for certain is, caring for a trailer park is not the meaning of life. Maybe it's the opposite, but I don't have time to sort through what is or isn't—I can only poke my head above the flurry of jobs for long enough to draw breath and remember the double asterisks. But even knowing it's there, I seem unable to get to it. I can't take it any longer. None of this is fair. I hate my grandma. I hate flipping burgers. I want my old life back.

On Sunday, when even the manager's jobs dip, I pick up my game controller, slip on my headset, and go on a gaming binge like I haven't in a week. I planned on an eight-hour play. For breakfast, I'd made a quadruple meal pot of KD. And I locked the trailer door.

I ignore the bangs that rattle the walls. The knocks. Tina's out there too, but Salminder will be helping her. Cleaning can wait. The pool can wait. Yes, even the cute, sad, pigtailed girl. In my game I'm campaign leader, wielding a diamond-tipped staff of power, riding a giant wolf against dragon spawn whose meaning of life is to end mine and my rangers' lives and then destroy our plane of existence—so I have an important job. One of my rangers is Chinese, two are from Los Angeles, there's a Canadian, a Brit . . . in all, I am guiding a score of rangers from a dozen countries in a joint mission to take down the Black Dragon that has kidnapped the king's daughters. Across the world another fifty spectators are following our progress as if it matters. Big stuff.

Skirmish after skirmish, we win. My spell casting ability grows until I pulse with power, and the rest of my team clatters with magical weapons, potions, and rods of impressive things. A cloak of near-invincibility flaps at my back, and I can teleport at will. After each dungeon level, I pause and muscle down another bite of orange goo. Now the Black Dragon throws spawn at us that are more fang and claw than anything else. We're way past the guard rooms and have cleared the Dragon Temple of its human acolytes. The traps have been evaded and secret passageways found. We're entering the nurseries of the Black Dragon—it's time to fry some lizard kids.

By the time the trailer shakes on its struts, I've advanced to High Wizard. The bone doors to the dragon's lair loom before me. Eighty-two spectators ping us with encouragement and strategies. The yelling beyond my headset is muted by exploding fireballs, clanging swords, and swearing in eight languages. Someone slides the window open beside my head and grabs my shoulder. I don't even look over, not at first; there are dragon spawn to consider and the rest of my party of heroes. In the trailer, the air has gone moist. The KD is three-quarters done and turned chewy dark, blood orange. Tina glares at me red-eyed with a look of jaw-clenched disappointment. My vision blurs, refocuses, eyes grainy with missed sleep. Her mouth opens and closes but I can't hear.

She rolls her eyes, disappears. I turn back to the screen but everything goes silent. The screen goes dark. I hear the snapping of twigs. Tina returns holding a bundle of pulled wires. She cut my power.

"I'm AWOL," I say. "My heroes."

"You're AWOL here, dork," Tina says. Then her eyes tear again.

"What's wrong?" I ask. "What's wrong with you?"

Her jaw flexes as if she's forcing something down. "Nothing, I'm covering your shifts, and you're a dork."

I frown and stand. My shirt actually crackles, it's so starched with old KD and sweat. Quickly, I swap it for a fresher T-shirt and stumble out into the light of day. "What time is it?"

"Afternoon," she says.

"I have to clean stuff," I groan.

"Wednesday."

"What? What Wednesday?" I ask.

"You've been in there for three days."

Oddly, my first thought is that if I played for one more day, I might have had a vision. Tina ruined my dork-vision-quest. To play video games until I found my avatar. I can imagine mine being a teeth-bared-in-fear emoji. I glance back at the trailer; someone has decorated it with toilet paper. Notes taped to the door by campers flutter in a breeze. A cicada buzzes. I'm ravenous. I need to pee.

"You really are a—"

I'm in a haze, but mumble, "A dork, I get it, thanks. Whatever."

On the air is the sweet smell of wood smoke and something I can't quite place. I follow Tina down the trail. Strewn about are pop cans and empty chip bags. At the trail's end bags of garbage crawl with maggots. A lumberjack huffs at me. The pigtailed girl looks on hopefully. I turn away. I'd rather that she glared.

In the washroom someone's yelling. "Mine!"

"It's mine!"

"I brought it myself."

"I need a square, just a square. Give it to me." The voice drops low and threatening.

I jog over and ease open the door to the women's washroom, about to ask what the matter is when I see a woman straddling another who is holding a roll of toilet paper over her head. They flip in muck. I shut the door quickly. The camp is ready to blow.

"Thanks for getting me," I say. But Tina shakes her head. "Listen, I'm sorry."

"Tell that to everyone else," she says, face flushing and eyes brimming.

"What?" I ask. I can tell something's up. "What is wrong?"

But she's gritting her teeth again.

"I don't need this crap," I reply, tired, hangry, and fed up. "You're the reason why I'm even doing this, you know?"

She wheels around. "For me?"

"Yeah, if I let my mom have the park, she's just going to sell it and then Pulled Beef will have to leave and—"

Her arms fold across her chest. "You're sure it's not about a million dollars? Don't do me any favors!" She starts to walk away. "Super dork!"

"Well, you're . . ." Pretty, smart, amazing, and "dork" hurts coming from her. "Not a very nice person."

She folds as if struck in the gut and kneels in the crusty road.

I jog over, but don't touch her. She's sobbing.

"Tina? I didn't mean it. You're nice. You're wonderful. I take it back."

She presses her hands over her ears.

"What's the matter?"

"My dad." Her chest hitches. "My dad's sick."

"What d'you mean?" I ask and then realize. "I'm sorry I missed my shifts. I'll take yours too, until he's better."

Tina looks to the sky and then her face crumbles. I bend and pull her into my shoulder. "Real sick . . . ," she says. "Cancer."

Salminder's the closest relation to me beyond my family. None of us have ever faced cancer, or anything close to it. It's not really something that computes. "I'm sorry, is he . . . okay?" I'm such an idiot, really a dork, but her sobbing stutters a bit. "I mean, they can do stuff, right?"

"They caught it, he says, but . . ."

And I know. *Cancer.*

A woman sprints out of the washroom, clutching the toilet paper roll like it's the Olympic torch. The second woman races after her. Suddenly I don't really care about how clean the campers' butts are. I don't care about virtual monsters, not when there's a real one right here in the park.

Tina says, "He doesn't want anyone to know." She's pale as she studies my face. "You deal with the camp. I'll start the grill. I'll see you later."

I don't know what to say. Over the last week, I'd jumped to the conclusion that Tina had suddenly become mean. I feel as though I've been pulled from an alternate reality and placed in a game that really blows. What can I do? But some games don't have a hack, a cheat. Not real-life games.

"I'm sorry," I reply, but Tina's already gone, and the women who were screaming about the toilet paper are looking expectantly at me.

Chapter 15

I suspect where the will is—in my mom's bedroom—but that's always locked when she's not around. There's only one time of day when I know her door is unlocked: night. While she's sleeping. Until then, I have three days of chores to catch up on.

I hand bomb toilet paper over the washroom stalls. Despite how crappy I've been, I even get a few cheers. The road is a ragged mess. Nothing can help it until there's another big rain. Obelix-the-camper stares at the hardened mud, his expression as droopy as the girl's at the pool-berg. Even knowing the ruts are going to be almost impossible to smooth out, I try anyway; chipping at clay's better than any of the other chores. I've disappointed everyone. I bail pool water into the washrooms and squeegee out the floors, which saves me at least an hour of scrubbing. Then I check in campers who, without me around, just grabbed spots and plugged in without paying. The camp is officially full, and it's not even July.

With a brain foggy from lack of sleep, I inspect the hot water heater and reignite the pilot. With a thump, the propane lights. The trailer park has hot water once more. I resist the urge to nap on the concrete floor. No one would find me there, but instead I head to the office and call Deneze, asking him to make a special run to get rid of the maggot factories.

From her lawn chair, my mom claps as I wander back and forth with pails of water. All the while I check over my shoulder to watch Tina fake-smiling at customers when I know all she wants to do is curl into a ball and cry. Somehow knowing the pain she's in makes it easier for me to power through my list. When I've done half my chores, I wad together the notes of camper complaints and jog to Pulled Beef.

Tina doesn't say anything when I take my place behind the grill. After a while the flames begin to blur. I struggle to stay awake. Smoke and heat wake me twice when I wait too long to flip a burger or lean too far forward. I make it through my shift, walk straight to my trailer, see the little girl standing in front of it while her mother raps on the door, and swerve into the forest. A hundred yards in, I lie down on a spongy mound of moss just on the edge of the swamp.

I planned only to wait them out. But I sink into a deep sleep.

***

By the chirps of insects and *garoumping* bullfrogs, I know it's night. But when I try to open my eyes, they won't. My fingertips tear at swollen eyelids, but they're inflamed by bug bites. The dark and me, we don't get along. My heart rate ramps. Fear slithers eel-like from the black waters to choke my throat.

One time, when I was four, I wandered out of the trailer to go for a wee. I must have gone too far into the woods because when I turned around the trailer had disappeared.

I'd cried for Mama, and Grandma, and Crystal. But when I heard the rustles of animals I screamed, turned, and sprinted into the arms of dead pine branches. Each scratch was a claw barely evaded, a tasting monstrous fang in my imagination. Soon swamp water rose to my knees, and I slowed with each sucking step. Panicked and only four years old, I didn't think about the swamp being away from camp. Only that I needed to keep moving and to escape.

Maybe I had imagined them, but eyes seemed to glow under a midnight fall moon. Shining yellow globes tracked me, but kept their distance, as if suspicious that I was bait for a hunter behind. But there was no hunter, just the snores of my family growing more distant by the step. To me the shining eyes were floating marbles. I could feel their menace but couldn't imagine to whom they belonged. Not until they howled. A howl to call the pack. And the pack replied.

Wolves. I couldn't count their number. I couldn't hear beyond my sucking footsteps and panting. I couldn't see the eyes anymore due to blurring tears. But I swear I spotted a cone of hot breath break the tree line bordering the swamp. The dark was so deep, so cold, and unrelenting.

In the swamp are large boulders, erratics left by the glacier's retreat. These are islands where the pines and birch grow in clumps. When the swamp water receded and my feet found dry land, I ran directly into one of the boulders and climbed. From the rock's height I reached the branches of a birch, and into its safety I clambered higher even as the wolves snuffled about the boulder. But the darkness still groped for me, and its cousin sleep threatened to drag me from the branches into slavering maws. All the dark long.

Early the next morning, Uncle Jamie found me. Staring, juddering with cold. He carried me back to my bed where I had fever dreams for two days before waking. I was safe, but never forgot the wolves howling at me in the dark, nor the bob of their marble eyes as they loped.

So, yeah, darkness is my greatest fear. And I can't even open my eyes, leaving my imagination to fill the woods with hooked-toothed watchers. My face feels bumpy and itchy as I lurch forward and straight into swamp. I spin, which is not a good idea, because I immediately lose my sense of direction. I stop to think and pry one eyelid open a crack until I spot a distant glow. As soon as I remove my fingers, my eyelids close again, so I can only take a dozen or so steps before I have to check again for the fuzzy light.

The water grows deeper for a moment and then levels out. With the throb of my heart in my ears, I can't even hear the slosh of my boots. The glow is a will-o'-the-wisp, luring me. Eventually the waters give way, but this is not the camp. It's a small island with an erratic the size of a house.

"Ray?" Uncle Jamie holds a long stick leveled at my chin. "Scared the heck outta me, what's the matter?"

"Woke up, can't see."

"Bug bites, all over yah," he says.

"Is it bad?"

Uncle pauses way too long. "Not like there's beauty contests for Mr. Sunny Days or nothing."

We tried an RV park pageant once, but the judging got political.

Uncle Jamie has mosquito netting over him. My vision's

fuzzed. The glow was from a fire burning so hot it's nearly white. Wood stacked to the side looks suspiciously like the wood I chopped.

"Wha'cha doing out here?" I ask, but he presses a cold can of pop on each of my eyes.

"You hold those and we'll get you back to bed."

He tugs the hem of my shirt and I follow, pressing the cool tin to my swollen eyelids. I'm comforted by him even though I stumble at times. We don't have to go back through the swamp, which is good because I'm sure I have a dozen leeches already.

By the time I reach the trailer, the swelling has gone down and I can see through slits.

"Should be better in the morning," Jamie says, leaving me with my hand on my trailer door. "Gotta run."

I blearily watch him head back the way we came.

Inside, I take a salt shaker and season the seven leeches suckling my calves and ankles. After the bugs and the leeches, I'm surprised I have any blood left. I shudder as the last falls to squirm on the floor. I wipe the muck from my legs and bury myself under a blanket.

My internal clock's off. I slept too early and too long. I toss and turn until 2:30 a.m.

Two-thirty's a special time in camp. The only time of day or night that someone isn't awake. Still, there are snuffles in the darkness, but everyone is at least trying to sleep. Except me. My eyes are better. Now's my chance: It's time to get the will back.

Problem is, I know Crystal sleeps with her gun. And if I wake my mom, she'll destroy or hide the will better, and I'll have to wait to get the will from Sam Peregrine. That won't happen today, and not in the foreseeable future. I'm running out of time. It seems worth the risk to try.

Panic curls its fingers around my throat as I scan the woods from the safety of my window, flashing my light to catch any eye shine.

There's none.

I ease the door of my trailer shut and slip into the night.

Chapter 16

Despite the cloud cover, I keep my flashlight pocketed. My feet know the way, and I reach the road and the first set of trailers. Some campers leave lights on all night, and the ambient glow is enough to keep me from tripping over the ridges of ruts. Once out of the darkness, I draw a deep breath and continue.

I pause at Tina's trailer. Her father washes it regularly and the siding glimmers. Wood is piled in a neat cord, stacked close but not too close to the fire pit. A screened-in area has small twinkling lights like stars. It's as if nothing has changed. As if everything's okay. I haven't spoken to Tina about her dad since she told me he has cancer. I don't know what to say. I don't know if I should ask. Would I want to chat? I think I'd want to forget and hope it went away. Maybe I don't want to know the answers. Because I care about him, and it hurts, and I don't want to add my pain to hers.

Someone coughs, and I hurry on to where floodlights pour down on the camp's front gates. Mom's trailer's dark. I still have a key from when I lived here a couple of years back. I cringe as I slide the key into the lock and turn. With a click, I pull on the lever. The door creaks wide.

I pause, breathe, and listen. Nothing. Not even a snore. I can only hear the steady hum of Grandma's brain freezer nearby. She would approve of this. Grandma always had a sparkle in her eye. It might have been the champagne.

The whole camper shifts as I step inside. I leave the door open. Crystal's hunting rifle's missing from the wall. When she's not mocking me, the bear's all she talks about. It's out there, waiting.

I shudder thinking about being out at night, stalking a grizzly. Could there be anything more terrifying than meeting a grizzly in the dark?

I put my sister's room at my back and head through the kitchen and dining area. The fridge rattles as it starts up and I nearly cry out, palm clapped over my mouth. It's a trailer so this all takes three seconds, and then I'm twisting the knob to my mother's door and easing inside. Her head's beneath the window. A side table is built into the corner beside her. The table's where she'll have stowed the will. She jerks forward, and I drop to the floor.

"Wha—wha . . . ?" Her lips smack.

A dream. She folds beneath her comforter. I start crawling backward to the door and escape. But I think of Tina and her dad, and the little pigtailed girl, Obelix, and jacks, and how it's almost been two weeks since Grandma died, two weeks since I cast that fateful fireball. I can't take it anymore. I need a solution. Okay, so it's really about me. The double asterisks could mean that I'm doing all this for nothing. A loophole. I can't have that sort of uncertainty.

I worm around the edge of the bed. Every couple of creaks—

there is no keeping anything secret in a trailer—I pause and listen for Crystal. My mom's breaths are steady and slow, ending with a whistle. I keep going. Finally, I lie flat before the side table. On my hands and knees I reach to open the drawer. It slides out, and I peer inside.

My mom grunts even as my fingertips brush cool papers. I turn my head.

She stares at me.

Her eyes flare.

"Whaaa!"

I scream too. She scrambles away like a crab until her hands slip off the side of the bed and she falls into the well between the bed and wood-paneled sidewall, feet kicking into the air and still screaming.

"Mama!" Crystal shouts from down the hall.

I reach into the drawer and snatch the will and stuff it into my shirt.

"It's me, it's Ray!" I cry over both.

The door opens. A gun barrel enters ahead of Crystal. She's got the rifle short stocked with the stock over her shoulder and her finger on the trigger.

"Ray, I'm Ray," I say.

She rubs up against the wall, and the light comes on.

Both of them gasp.

"It's a monster," my mom says.

They're both naked, but I can't shut my eyes with a gun pointed at my chest.

"What d'you do with my brother?" Crystal cries.

I glance at the mirror on the wall. It's with a mix of horror and understanding that I see the bubbly mass of my face.

"Oh, no, no, it's only bug bites."

"Shoot it," my mom says. "Put it out of its misery."

Crystal looks like she's about to but then stops. "No such thing as monsters, Mama. Those're skitter bites." The barrel dips—a little. "Why you here, Ray?" Crystal asks.

I think fast.

"Malaria," I say. "And West Nile Virus. Zika too."

"You got all of 'em?" my mom asks.

"Giving me fever dreams," I say. "Sleepwalking."

Crystal's eyes narrow. "What was you keeping in your table there, Mama?"

My mother's managed to pry herself back onto the bed, and she leans over to inspect the empty drawer.

"I was looking for . . . an antidote. For the diseases," I say. "And what do you have against pajamas?"

"Give me back the will, son." My mother says it cold as the pool-berg.

I'm skinny. I can't take my stronger sister in a fight. I can't take my mom. But I have sense. And I *am* skinny.

I drop to the floor and wriggle beneath the bed.

"Get 'im!" they shout together.

I don't stop wriggling until I'm right under the middle of the queen-size bed with only enough room to slip out the will and shine my flashlight. I flip right to the end of the will. I find the double asterisks.

**To give Ray a fighting chance I have hired Dalen Anders, Motivational Guru to the Rich and Famous, to join him for the month. If Ray doesn't need him then Dalen's pay will be kept in the *estate. He sounded really good on TV, though. Call to arrange.*

I don't care that they have my feet or that my stomach is burning from the rug as they rip me from underneath the bed. I now understand why my mother wanted to keep the will from me. I have a secret weapon. A game hack. A man who already knows the meaning of life. A guru Grandma will pay to tell me the answer.

Chapter 17

I slept the rest of the night on the couch, not trusting my mother to open the door for me in the morning. We're far enough north here that no cell phones work. Our Internet is on satellite and the phone line is a fragile connection that usually goes out with any sort of wind, ice, or snow. This is the only place for me to call my savior.

My mom sags into the couch springs as I make the call.

"It's real money you're burning there," she says. "My money."

"Grandma's," I say and point through the window to the head of her statue. "She's still there."

"It's not! She's not! That's a frozen brain."

"Dalen Anders's office," a man announces, and I grin.

I look back at my mom, who watches with red-rimmed eyes. Crystal shakes her head. "Everything handed to you," she says. "Go ahead, you can't do nothing on your own, so why's this any different."

"Yes—It's Ray," I say into the phone. "My grandma told me to give you a call if I needed help. Georgia Saintbury?"

"This the RV Park Queen?" he replies. "Or the new king, I guess, right?"

"Well, I dunno about—"

"One minute while I transfer you."

I wait in silence as thick as the muddy road ruts. My mom's lips are white from pursing.

"Fine, three thousand dollars," she blurts. "Three thousand dollars if you hang up right now. I'll take back the park and we call it a day. Promise not to sell until the end of the summer."

"Ray? Ray?" The voice on the other end of the receiver crackles with energy. "Hey, hey! Are you ready to learn the meaning of life?"

"You know you can't do it," Mom says. "You jes' spent three days playing on a computer and near ruined the park. As if you can handle the rest of the month."

"Yeah, 'sides, no one knows the meaning of *yer* life. No one," Crystal adds.

If Dalen hadn't spoken again just then, I would have hung up. I'd have gotten what I wanted. If my mom hadn't said I couldn't do it with such certainty, I would have hung up. Because, despite mostly believing her, there is a tiny part of me that thinks it's possible for me to figure it out. If I hang up now, I'd have my money. Enough to start somewhere else and to spend a couple of weeks gaming. Tina would be okay, and I'd have my life back. But what life is that? If there is one thing I've learned for certain so far, it is that I don't know the meaning of life.

"Raymond?" Dalen asks. "You there? Are you ready?"

"Three thousand dollars, and a two-week vacation," Mom

says. "Won't bother you at your trailer. You're not going to find the meaning of life."

I hope that, with all the swelling, she can't see the stinging tears in my eyes. Out the window, Tina walks by, and I wonder what she'd do.

"Think about it," my mom adds. "Sleep on it."

Another night. This can't wait another night.

"Yes, sir," I say into the phone. I've already wasted half the month. "I'm ready."

"I'll be there in, let me check Google Maps . . . eight hours and fifteen minutes. Where the heck are you, geez?"

I'm about to say thank you, but there's a click and dial tone.

"He'll be here tonight," I say.

"Don't see why he couldn't tell you the meaning of life over the phone," Crystal replies.

"Better go clean your toilets," Mom snarls.

A weight lifts from my chest. Someone is coming who knows. An adult, a *guru*, who has the answers. I can breathe. The gut-berg even seems to melt and flip. I can clean toilets.

As I collect the rags and pail, I see that the pool-berg on top of the pool cover has melted to the size of a refrigerator. I take that as a sign. Chains screech on metal as pigtailed girl kicks her legs out and back on the swing. As she does, one rust-flecked leg of the swing set lifts and lands, lifts and lands. I wave at her. She grins back. I don't deserve it and find it amazing that she could be happy here. Friendless in a filthy camp with so little to do. Two of her front teeth are missing. I can't remember the last time I smiled so big someone could count my teeth. Do children know the meaning of life and then forget it? Or are they too young to have to worry about it?

I'd been happy before Grandma died. Hadn't I?

I fill the pail with water and begin mopping out the stalls, running the gray water over toilet seats, counters and sinks until it at least looks clean. Then I change the water and scrub out the showers. As I do, something drools on my shoulder. Long tendrils of goo hang from the ceiling. I shudder, swallow the bit of bile in my throat, and swing the mop up to attack the snotties.

None of this bothers me. I'm imagining what I'll do with a million dollars.

I'll rent an apartment. Set up the fastest Internet connection known to humanity, and game for years. Pizzas will appear at my door for each meal. Across the world hundreds of thousands will watch me game. I won't be a High Wizard. I will be the *Supreme Wizard*, and the ancient red wyrm coiled at the center of the world will fall under my thrall.

Seven hours and four minutes remain. Sam Peregrine will be back in her office soon, too. With any luck, by this time next week I'll be explaining to her the meaning of life, with time to spare.

A half hour later, I'm scraping at crunchy tire ruts, trying to fill the deepest of them, and giving up when my shoulders begin to burn and blisters reopen on my palms. Next is fielding camper complaints. Each camper stumbles back when they see my plagued face.

"My neighbor, that trailer there." The jack points at a small trailer with a canvas awning. "He's a late shifter at the mines, and every night when he gets home it's like he's trying to do a light show or something because there's all this flashing."

I stand and nod. "Maybe ask him to stop?"

"That's what you're for," he says. "I'm not getting out of bed at midnight to argue. Is that leprosy you got?"

I make a note and continue down the line.

"Washing machine ate my quarters," another older man says, covering his mouth as if my bug bites could be contagious.

I promise him a dollar and keep going to the next complaint.

"Dryer stole my sock."

"That's what dryers do, I think," I say and lift my jeans to show two crusty socks, one gray, one whitish.

"No, they don't."

I promise him a sock. Six hours, some odd minutes until the meaning of life. There are six more complaints. No one's worried about the pool, but I skip the little girl's trailer and go straight to poolside to see what I can do about it.

With a long stick I poke the berg. You know how they say the part of the iceberg that's showing is only ten percent of the whole? Well the refrigerator on top is hiding the pickup truck-sized hunk beneath the cover. Leaves clutter the pool, and the rubber cover is torn but finally free of ice. I haul it to the side. The pool at least looks more like a pool because the blue liner bottom offers a false reason for optimism, but, if anything, the problem seems worse because the cover had been hiding yet more ice. The pigtailed girl takes a flying leap off the swing and tears away to her trailer. I drag the remains of the cover to the dumpster and feed it over the sides. Then I empty the rest of the garbage cans around camp and pile the bags one after the other into the bin.

There's a squeal and pigtails flap as the little girl, now wearing her bathing suit, races to the pool and then stands sad-faced, staring at the pool-bergs. Swim goggles hang from her fingers. I duck when she turns, and I sneak around trailers and come up on Pulled Beef from the other side to take my evening shift.

"Hiding from a little girl?" Tina asks as I enter.

"Don't want to frighten her with my face," I reply. "Besides, swimming isn't as much fun as it sounds."

"Ah, so you're protecting her from the disappointment of the joy of swimming pools, how good of you," Salminder says, face smiling beneath an orange turban.

I didn't see Salminder with the fridge door open, and stare at him now. What do I say?

"And death by drowning—why take the risk, right?" Tina adds. "If you opened the pool, that would mean she could swim, and that kind of fun can result in all sorts of injuries."

I need to respond, but I can't say anything. Tina said Salminder doesn't want anyone to know. But I'm sad, too. The silence stretches as Salminder's smile fades.

"Why orange?" I ask quickly. "The turban."

The smile grows again. "It has great significance in the Sikh religion," he replies.

"Really? Why's that?"

"It goes very well with my shirt."

"Oh," I say and inspect the toes of my boots.

"Tina told you," he says.

"I'm sorry, Daddy." Tina touches him on the shoulder in a way that I don't remember my mother touching me.

"It's okay, Sunlight," he says. "I am glad."

We lapse into silence, but not the sort of efficient silence of the past where we're all working as a team. This is another of those awkward dividing silences. We serve lines of jacks and a couple of the survivalists who flit in whenever the line's gone and disappear again.

"How's your mother?" Salminder asks as dusk and mosquitoes settle over the park.

"Okay," I reply. "Not dying of anything."

Tina drops her knife.

"Sorry," I say.

Tears shimmer in Tina's eyes.

"*Are* you dying?" I ask. Emotion clamps greasy fingers around my heart.

"We're all dying." Salminder grins again, and I don't know how he can.

"Yeah, but . . ."

"Some of us sooner than we'd like?" His smile isn't quite so broad.

Tina's standing there with her eyes and mouth open wide. I don't even know if she's asked these questions yet.

"Cancer," Salminder says. "Will shorten my life, most likely. But I cannot let that stop me, or you, or my Tina from living."

"This guy, Dalen Anders, is coming today, should be here soon," I say. "Maybe he can help you too?"

"Wait. The guy from TV?" Tina asks.

"I'd never heard of him," I say. "But I think so."

"Why would he come here?" She seems way too excited by this.

"He's going to tell me the meaning of life," I reply. Salminder laughs.

"He's *big*, Dad. He once cured someone of their fear of flying in five minutes."

"Fear is nothing to be afraid of," Salminder replies. "Letting it control you is the problem."

"Yes, Dalen said that, too. The guy went on to learn how to fly a plane." There's a light back in Tina's eyes. I don't know if it's because Salminder seems so okay with dying and all, or maybe she's starstruck by celebrity.

There's sudden cheering and a big whooping shout over a megaphone.

"Who can do it?" demands the voice.

"You can!" replies the crowd.

And more clapping.

"When the student is ready, the teacher arrives," Salminder says.

I hesitate at the door. An hour remains of my shift, but the line for food has vanished.

There's another cheer.

"Go on." Salminder waves me off. "You owe me an extra—"

I'm out of Pulled Beef before he can finish.

Chapter 18

The ribbed shell of a massive bus gleams in the setting sun. As I rush closer, the eyes of a gigantic head with a silver mane coalesce and stare down from an image on the side of the bus before a crowd of campers off shift. In the door of a bus that probably cost as much as the entire campground stands Dalen Anders. His eyes are the same intense dark as his photo's; if anything they're brighter, and the silver hair gives his skin the glow of burnished copper.

He wears electric blue jeans and a white, ruffled silk shirt on a lean frame as he shouts, "Now someone tell me how one finds Ray, the RV Park King."

There's epic silence.

My mother cackles.

Someone asks, "You mean, Swami Ray? He's here somewheres."

Dalen's smile broadens as he shakes his head. "Not here, this man's worth probably in the order of a billion, a few hundred million at the very least. I got turned around somewhere back at . . . sorry, I blinked and missed the town, know what I mean? Where's Sunny Days' executive offices?"

My mother hoots and hoots. "A *billion*!"

"Yes, ma'am," Dalen says with a measure of awe. "I've never seen an elderly lady like that eat so much caviar, like it was another food group."

"You've come to the right place." Crystal points at the statue. "There's yer lady. Old coot."

Dalen's smile falters.

I'm pushing through the crowd, hand halfway up. "I . . . me . . . I'm Ray."

"All hail, King Ray!" my mother shouts, and there's scattered laughter.

"You're Dalen Anders? It was me on the phone."

His name's printed on the bus and beneath it, *Who can? You can!*

"Ray," Dalen states but pulls me up to his side, smiling again for pictures. "Got something of a skin condition there, don't you?"

The way he grins, I keep looking for a television crew, but there isn't one. "My grandma hired you," I say.

"It's a real pleasure to meet you, Ray. It is a real pleasure." He shakes my hand. "How old are you? Twelve?" he asks, not unkindly.

Crystal and Mom are clutching each other, holding themselves upright, tears of laughter streaming down their faces.

"Seventeen," I say. "You're in the right place."

Realization seems to dawn on Dalen. He claps his hands together and he leans back. "Of course, you're a coder, aren't you? Write software out of a trailer, an eccentric. What's your social network? Surprised I haven't heard of it." I shake my head.

"Campy YouTube videos then, millions of followers online." Dalen's smile cracks as Crystal's piercing glee rings out. "So who are you, kid? Why am I here?"

"I'm Ray. Just Ray. I need the meaning of life so I can inherit the RV park." My arm takes in the swath of the park. "Sunny Days."

Dalen glances around as if for the first time. Looks back and nods at the big sign over the park entry. "This RV park. This is the *only* park? Not a hundred of these across the country or something? The McDonald's of RV parks?" It's like he keeps digging as if there's gold here if he can only just find it.

"Nope. Just the one."

Dalen slaps his forearms where a mosquito has bitten through the silk. The corpse leaves a red smudge on his shirt. The guru stares as if it's a gunshot wound.

"I'm afraid there has been some sort of mistake," Dalen says, evidently coming to the conclusion that there's nothing but bugs here.

"I don't think so. You help people figure out their lives, right?" The joy I'd felt at his arrival is quickly departing. Tina squints at Dalen. Everyone's watching. There are even a few phones out recording.

"Yeah, but, kid, I help billionaires. Not little—"

I step right in front of him. "I need help. I don't know what to do."

"With what? A bear problem?" Dalen smiles at his own joke.

Mom gasps. "Bear got Grandma."

"Didn't mean it as an insult," he says with a wave and leans down, but still doesn't set foot on camp soil. "Listen, if you let this go, I won't sue you for misrepresentation."

"Mis—" I scratch my head.

"False pretenses. Your grandma, I thought she was rich. Really rich," his speech jutters.

"You mean, you assumed she was," I say, folding my arms over one another. I'm struggling, because part of me never wants to see this man again, but the other half of me says you don't get as rich as he obviously is without being good at your job. I need him.

"I won't sue," he repeats.

"You can't help me?" I ask.

He jerks back as if I've delivered a jab. "I didn't say I can't help you, Ray."

I look down.

"You won't then," says Obelix.

The crowd of jacks press in tighter as the conversation grows quieter. Dalen's eyes roll.

The guy smiles for the cameras. Even Crystal and my mother glower.

"I tell you what. I'll cut you half my fee back." He pulls a checkbook from his jacket, scribbles in it, and presses the check into my palm.

"Who can do it?" he intones, but it's half-hearted and results in silence. "Wow, actual crickets," he mutters and backs up the stairs of the bus. "Get us the hell out of here," he says to the driver.

There's a brief muffled argument and then the door shuts. The bus starts to reverse down the drive.

"Well, wasn't he a pea-brained peacock?" my mom says.

My double asterisks back toward the sunset.

Chapter 19

The bus has no room to turn around, so it slowly bumps backward down the road. In the windshield Dalen stands watching.

Tina taps me on the shoulder.

"He's a jerk," she says and then her eyes widen. "Holy—I gotta become a motivational speaker!"

She's pointing to the check; on it is a number followed by more zeroes than I've ever seen. Fifty thousand dollars. Word of the amount ripples through the crowd.

Mom starts shouting at Grandma for spending her money. I can't take my eyes away from the bus as it nears a bend.

"Take the money, bro," Crystal says. "You were never going to figure out the meaning of life, this is more than you'd ever get from Mom, and she's not going to give you nothing now you went and lost the other half of that."

And then I understand. In my hand is a check for *half* the amount Dalen Anders charges for coaching. Half. If I take this check, I burn through fifty thousand dollars. But if I don't take the check and can convince Dalen to stay, I'll have to spend two weeks with that guy and will have probably wasted a hundred thousand anyway.

A tree branch groans and snaps as the bus brushes it. Like everywhere around here, the swamp isn't far from high ground, and the tires run perilously close to the ditch. The phone and power lines go down, the generator kicking in on Grandma's brain. And I see it, swinging in the front of the bus windshield, at times obscuring Dalen's face: a dream catcher.

A sign.

I start to walk.

"What are you—?" Crystal demands as I pass under the park gate.

I start to jog. The rear of the bus is around the bend. I wave my arms and run as fast as I can. The bus accelerates. Dalen gesticulates at the driver, who keeps her eyes on the side mirror. My lungs burn and I stumble, scrape a shin, and scramble to run again.

It must have hit a still muddy patch because the bus stops and then starts rocking back and forth. I rush up to the grill as the engine roars. I hold the check up high. Dalen's eyes widen. I tear the check into shreds. The bus surges forward out of the muddy gully, hits me, and I fly back a dozen feet. My skull thwacks into the road. The bumper roars up over my legs. If it weren't for all the mud and the ruts, I'd have been squashed, but the driver's already got it in reverse and the bus worms as it backs right off the road and into the ditch. Pieces of fifty thousand dollars flutter about.

"What the hell were you—?" Dalen launches off the bus, his expression twisting as he skids to my side.

"I'll kill ya, I'll kill ya, I'll kill ya." It's like a murderous train chugs behind me. It's coming from camp, but my vision swims. "I'll kill ya, I'll kill ya!"

"Are you okay?" Dalen manages before the train barrels past, catches him beneath his chest bone, and he sails backward to land in the muck.

He cries as my mother rains fists from above.

I reach down and press my hands along my legs, which lie within a wheel rut. There's no pain. I pull up my pants and stare at the tire tread marks. I yank my legs out of the mud. I've been run over by a bus but I'm fine. Just fine. Watching my mother hammer away at the little semi-enlightened man, a lightness fills me.

Dalen and my mom scream at one another as I climb to my feet, legs quaking.

"You owe me one month," I say over him. "My grandma paid already."

"Misrepresent—" he starts, but my mother holds a fist cocked.

"One month, and I won't sue for hitting me with your bus."

"You people are insane!" he shouts and rolls from beneath my mother to his knees.

The bus keeps digging itself deeper into the swamp beyond the road. Without a tow, it's not going anywhere.

"One month," I repeat. "Two weeks, actually. That's all I have time for anyway."

He looks from my mom to the angry campers and back to me.

Behind him, the bus honks, and the driver lifts her hands in surrender. "All right, fine, all right, let's do this. How hard can it be? What's the meaning of life for a seventeen-year-old? Video games and girls, right?"

He hesitates in the silence, brushing as much caked mud as he can from his shirt. The campers close in on us, and he takes a step backward toward the bus. "Why don't you come on up, Ray? Get started." Glancing uncertainly from the campers to me, he motions to the bus door, which the driver opens. "Are you ready to change your life?" His smile flickers.

Even though Dalen's tone lacks conviction now, I take a deep breath and follow him aboard. I *so* am.

Chapter 20

"Ray, meet Charlie." It's a despondent intro. Dalen keeps picking at a shirt obviously ruined.

Charlie, the bus driver, gives an uncertain wave. She has short blonde hair and blue searching eyes. My ears are ringing from the hit, and my back's scratched from the fall. It's then I realize why she's so pale. She's worried I'm about to keel over.

"I'm okay," I say as everything swings left and then right. I struggle to hold my head still. "I think."

Dalen takes my elbow and drags me to a couch, first covering it in a towel before letting me sit. Out the tinted window my mother hisses up at the bus. Crystal's joined her with a gun at her back.

I smile despite myself.

"Relax, have a soda," Dalen says. He's disappeared into a back room. The motor coach is one giant RV, but decked out with leather and inlaid wood. The kitchen has granite counters and a full-size fridge. When he returns, Dalen's wearing a cotton T-shirt. The mud has been washed from his face. An angry bruise rises at his chin.

"Normally I'd dress a bit better, but just in case that woman . . ." He trails off, brushing nonexistent dirt from his shoulder. "So, tell me about yourself."

I'm woozy. "Ray, short for Raymond. You met my mom, and the one with the gun's Crystal, my sis. I'm seventeen."

Dalen leans in. "What do you do, Ray?"

"I have a job. Flip burgs."

"Burgs?"

"Burgers."

"Ah, hamburgers. Organic? Grass fed? Is it a chain—Never mind." He shakes his head. "Why am I here, again?"

I'm pretty sure he's trying to convince himself. "If I can figure out the meaning of life, I get the campground. At least until Grandma resurrects."

"Resurrects?" he asks.

"Yeah, her brain's cryogenically frozen. She thinks we'll have technology in the future to bring her back." I point out the window toward Grandma.

"Something to research." He glances back to Charlie, who rolls her eyes. "But, Ray, I can't tell you the meaning of life."

Here I was going to call Sam Peregrine for an appointment. The ice in my stomach. Maybe it had been there before Grandma died and playing video games helped me forget about it. But I recognize it now. It's a block of panic. The meaning of the double asterisks and then the possibility of Dalen's wisdom had held it in check. Now that panic freezes everything around it. It sends icy bits into my veins. My heart thunders. This jerk gets a hundred thousand dollars and I get . . . nothing? How can I face my mom? How can I face Tina or Crystal?

"What d'you mean? That's what my grandma's paying you for," I manage. "The meaning of life."

Dalen shakes his head. "You don't get it. Usually, my job's to help people rediscover their *lost* meaning of life. But there's nothing to work with here. If you were a genius who lost his creative touch, or a mega billionaire who lost their work-life balance and forgot their kids' birthdays all the time, I'd have the magic you need. The people I fix were once great. They go on to change lives around them. You're gonna, what? Gonna rearrange how people park their trailers?"

There's a flash of light followed by *Kaboom!* a moment later.

"What was that?" Charlie asks.

"My uncle. Fireworks," I mumble.

"So now that you understand, what d'you say? Fifty grand, we forget about the whole bus accident, and I'll throw in the complete collection of my books and quotes." He reaches beneath the coffee table and pulls out a stack, and places them on top. "That's like another two hundred bucks, but reviewers say they're priceless—you *can* read?"

"You're giving up on me?" I ask.

"Giving up?" He chuckles a little. "Look, little man, I have one life to live, too. I'm not the one searching for meaning here. I can help people who change things or I can help people who can't. There's a difference. Economies of scale. People like you read my books."

"You can't help me." I sink into the couch.

This gets Dalen's attention. "Sure, I can help you. I choose not to."

My headache's growing worse. "I think I have a concussion."

"You'd be a snap. I just don't want to be selfish. I have a choice to make. I can help one kid who will stay in this place, or I can help someone rich and powerful who might control the destinies of thousands of others."

I sag, folding my arms across my chest. "You're right. I don't have money. I'm not a genius. I'm just average—maybe not even that. You've never helped average, have you? Why should I bother?"

Dalen's eyes tighten, and he swallows hard. "I can help you through my books. My books have helped millions. Have you read the comments beneath my videos?"

"So you're a rock star, whatever, but have you ever coached someone average? Below average? Is there even a point?"

"Why would anyone average pay a hundred grand to be coached by me?"

A hundred thousand dollars. I still can't believe it myself. "You must be really good," I say and smile sadly.

He grumbles and shares a look with Charlie, who's frowning at him and giving nudging nods.

"Look. Why do you want my help?" he asks.

"I told you, if I figure it out I get the RV park."

He shakes his head. "Then I actually can't help you."

His checkbook is back out, and with it a pen.

"At the start," I add slowly, "I didn't want the park. Then, I thought about how my grandma wanted me to have it. My sister and mom became so mean, so then I wanted to kick them out. To show them I could do it. But then there was Tina and Uncle Jamie too, and what would they do?"

"For money or revenge, you're really missing the point of it, kid." Dalen chuckles.

"Dalen," Charlie warns, and his smile drops.

"Okay, what about now?" he asks.

"Now, I guess it's because I feel totally lost. When I started to work on the park, I saw how a whole life could be spent running from one chore to the next. It was all laid out, and if I don't start doing the right things I'll never figure anything out. Won't have the time to change." That gut-berg panic crackles. I suck in deep breaths before calming. "It's funny, but when I tore up the check, that was when I really decided I wanted to know the answer. Will you help me?" I squeak. "I want—I want to be better."

"No fifty grand? *Fifty thousand dollars?*"

"Nope."

"Make it sixty, high as I can go. I had to cancel a show for this."

I shake my head. His dark eyes seem to burrow into me.

"Dalen," Charlie urges. "This could be just the thing. What we talked about."

The guru clucks his tongue at her and then clears his throat. I jerk back when his palms slap his thighs. "You know what? I'll do it. Fresh air. Kind of a vacation for me."

I swallow. "You'll help me?"

Charlie breaks into a dazzling smile. Dalen waves her off. "I'll help you help yourself."

I shudder a little, seeing now how this wasn't going to come easy. He wasn't going to let me in on the secret so fast.

"Are you ready? Are you *sure* you're ready? Not for money. Not for spite, or for love even, but for *you*."

I nod.

It's like a switch is flipped. He runs manicured fingers through glossy rich hair that a lion would be proud of.

"Call me 'Coach'," he says with these eyes that demand my attention.

"Yes, sir," I say. "*Coach.*"

"Good." He claps and I jump. "You are an Olympic athlete and I am your trainer."

"Me?" I say.

"You. We're going to use secret techniques. You are the CEO and I'm your venture capitalist. I am Obi-Wan Kenobi and you're Luke Skywalker. Are you ready? Are YOU ready!?" His hands grip my shoulders. He's farther into my personal space than Tina's ever gone.

"Yes?"

"Yes! We're going to rekindle the spark that you've lost!"

I blink. "Seriously, Coach, there never was a spark."

He stumbles a bit and then nods. "You need to figure out what your life is about before it's too late. You're in crisis!"

Panic crystallizing in my blood. *Yup.*

"Soon people will start telling you that you look younger."

"Um, great?"

"An aura of power will surround you and your steps will thunder." He's shaking my shoulders back and forth and my brain sloshes with it. "Together we will find your soul. Today is the first day of your new life. Who can do it?" He pauses, and I realize I'm supposed to say something.

"I . . . can?"

"Louder." He pumps a fist.

"I can."

He waves his arms.

"I can!" I shout and then cringe from the pain in my head.

"Only those who seek shall find, my friend. You're a seeker—I can see it in your eyes." He holds me still for a long moment, hands back at my shoulders, and his gaze mining mine. "You know what? I don't think you're average at all, kid. Not average at all."

Chapter 21

"So, what are your goals?" Dalen asks later, when my headache's subsided.

"You tell me," I say, leaning forward and rubbing my hands together, crumbly mud flaking from my skin. I fight the urge to itch at my face. He sits beside me now, our foreheads nearly touching.

He looks at me oddly. "What do you mean—*you tell me*? What are you expecting with this?"

I glance to Charlie and then back to Dalen's fierce stare.

"Uh, I actually thought you'd tell me the meaning of life, maybe it would take a few days, and then I was going to go to the lawyer and tell the lawyer, and then we could all go home."

"And now? Are you still not getting it? You know I cannot tell you the meaning of life. I can only help you to discover it for yourself."

This panic-berg, it bobs against my insides, freezing where it touches.

"Yeah, it's going to be different. Secrets and all," I say and lean back against the armrest.

On the wall beside the small couch there's a photo of Dalen with his arm around a young girl. A woman stands behind the pair, in the picture, but not quite all in. Dalen follows my eyes.

"My daughter," he says, and I know by the omission that the woman isn't at all in the picture anymore. He slaps his leg, and I jerk. "One step at a time. Set a goal for today, Ray. Achieve it. Say, no drugs today. No hookers. No more online gambling." I frown. "You can do it! We will use the secrets of ancients. I've studied from the masters. When you know the goal for the day and then the week, you can learn the goal for the month. When you know the goal for the month, you can set your sights on the year. Those who have the foresight of one year can know their destiny."

"I don't do drugs," I say.

"Achievement unlocked, we can work on the hookers. Don't wait for someone to make your day. Winners make their own days!"

"Where do I start?" I ask.

"Who says we haven't?" From the back of his pocket he pulls a journal, opens it and hands it over.

Day 1, reads the first page.

"Write down today's goal."

I sit there and then write: *Figure out the meaning of life.*

Dalen looks over my shoulder. "No, no, no, that's not what I mean. That's the destiny. With one eye on the destination you only have one eye for today. What happens if you walk around with one eye closed? If you concentrate on the endgame it will take you twice as long to get there, because you will lack focus on the now."

I wrestle with what he's saying. Dalen begins pacing up and down the length of the bus.

"How are you going to make your day good? What does a good day look like? It has to be achievable," he says.

"No one's yelling at me? I can game."

Dalen draws another deep breath and then lifts a finger as if he's got the solution. "What do you have to do to stop people yelling at you?"

"Make everyone happy."

"By . . . ?"

"Cleaning the washrooms, and the road needs to be fixed, the pool, plus the playground's a deathtrap. Now the power's out and the phone because of the bus, and I still have my shifts at Pulled Beef." I can feel the blood drain from my face. *Salminder's dying.* I keep forgetting and then remembering all over. Beneath the surface, gut-berg's bigger than I'd imagined. "I can't do it all. I can't, I just can't."

The corners of my mouth wrench down and I can't stop them either. My eyes blur with tears.

"Worry, worry, worry. Most of the stuff we worry about never happens. Worry is a symptom that you live too much in the future. You can't afford negative thoughts, not a one. Not a single bad one about yourself or about anyone else."

"I can't do that—they just pop into my head."

He sits beside me and takes my hands. It's weird because I can't remember the last time a man, a person of any kind, has touched me in so intimate a way. It's not sexual or anything, it just doesn't happen to me. I cringe from it, but he holds.

"They don't *pop* into your head." Dalen's intense eyes hardly blink. "You control them. If there's anything I can teach you, it's that. Only you are in control of your thoughts. Thoughts lead to actions, actions to habit, habit to destiny. In fact, my friend, your thoughts are the *only* thing in your control." I blink away tears and manage to flatline my mouth again. "Listen, say your boss doesn't give you a promotion . . ."

I'm shaking my head and even manage a small laugh. I can't tell if he's trying to be funny or really so out of touch with what it means to be seventeen in a campground. "Like head burger flipper?"

"That's not really your world, huh?"

"Nope."

"Say your girlfriend . . . you have a girlfriend?" I shake my head again. He has nothing to work with. "Imagine you do, and she cancels a date. What's your initial thought?"

"Maybe she doesn't like me anymore?" I shrug.

"And how would you feel about that?" The questions come right on top of my answers as if he's gone through this patter so many times.

"Sad, angry," I say.

"Right, good. But maybe she's sick? Maybe it's an opportunity to go deeper with her? Instead of texting an angry message back you say, 'Are you okay? What's wrong? What can I do to make your life easier?'"

Salminder and Tina. She's not the one who's sick, but I see it. Maybe they don't need silence right now? Maybe my stupid questions earlier were exactly what they had needed? And maybe her anger was less directed at me and more due to worry over her father. I sit up.

"I can tell you got part of that."

I release a deep breath.

"Manage your mind, manage your life. I'll help you with this evening's goal. It's a hard one, maybe the hardest. For tonight I want you to become aware of your thoughts. Catch yourself if you think a negative one and write it down here." He taps the book. "Go ahead, write the goal down."

I do. *Write down negative thoughts.*

"Good, that's it. Now go on, sounds like you've got some stuff to do."

Chapter 22

I stumble down the steps of the bus. Run-over, bug-eaten, and reeling a bit from everything he'd said, I hold his books in my arms. Everyone has long ago dispersed. I've missed most of my evening shift at Pulled Beef, and Tina's going to be annoyed. Everyone's conspiring against me. *Crap*. Now I have to write that stupid thought down. *Crap,* that one too.

I'm standing between the bus and Sunny Days. The park looms like a mountain of chores.

Do I really need to go through with this? I mean, it's not like I *have* to.

Grandma stares down at me. A hundred thousand dollars. That's how much this is costing. Whether it's money I won't get at the end of the month or money Uncle Jamie and my mom will never see, my mom was right: it's real money.

I'll write my evil thoughts down. See where it takes me. Transcribing thoughts for the rest of the evening doesn't really seem like a good way to figure out what I should be doing with the rest of my life, but whatever.

Write that one down, too.

Smoke trails from around my uncle's firework shack. The sun's still up and will be for another couple hours.

As I walk through Sunny Days' gate, my mom shouts, "So, what's the meaning of life there?"

I pause for a second. Glance around. It's not here.

I shake my head and scratch at a particularly big bite.

"I knew it," is all she says and ducks back into her trailer.

I'm about to shout back but swallow it. Crystal's laughter pierces the moldering vinyl camper walls.

I lug the books to Pulled Beef. The line's a half dozen deep. Manageable for one person. Inside the grill sizzles and flares under Tina's expert hands. This is time she could be spending with her father, and I've made her stay here.

"I'm sorry," I say, dumping the books on the floor of the trailer, putting on a hair net and apron. "I'll take over and close." Tina's blank, uncaring look terrifies me. Grief has tarnished her eyes. I've seen the dullness in others. I've felt it myself. But not her. Sunlight's in shadow. "It'll get better," I say.

"So you've got all the answers now?" she replies, slamming the spatula on the grill so that it bounces and grease sprays the aluminum foil taped on the wall.

"Didn't mean—"

"Forget it," she says. "Stop trying to make me feel better or pretending it's fine."

I flush. How's it going to get better for her? How? When her father dies?

As she pushes through the door, I lean out past the jack holding out his five bucks and call to her. "How can I help you?" I say, repeating Dalen. "How can I make your life easier?"

There's a hitch in her step and then she shouts back, "Keep your shifts."

I hesitate. "Sorry, running the camp and the whole Dalen thing . . . ," I say.

She stops and then pretends to shoot people in a video game. "Pew, pew, pew . . . ," she says, and then walks on.

I don't even like first-person shooter games.

The worst customer is the pigtailed girl. Not because she whines at me about the pool, but because she doesn't. She smiles and doesn't mention it as if she's used to my answers by now. *Sorry, nothing I can do, little girl. It's a big chunk of ice. Soon.*

It's dark by the time I walk back to my trailer. I spent another hour trying to chip mud back into the ruts. The swelling in my face has subsided, and I no longer feel as though I want to scratch off my cheeks. Light shines from the corners of Uncle Jamie's shack. He hadn't been making fireworks for a week, not while he fed his swamp fire. He seems to be making up for lost time. In my trailer I pull a ball of socks from a laundry basket. I stuff the socks into a pocket and then grab a dollar from where I keep my money in a little lockbox. There's not much there; I spend most of it on new games or upgrades to my gear.

I ate a Ray Special for dinner—one of the perks of the job—and so have time to go drop the socks and the dollar by the campers. On the light-show guy's trailer, I post a note asking for him to hood his lights at night so as not to disturb others. Sock guy thanks me, but his eyes water when he sniffs the pair; lost-dollar dude says he would have preferred quarters. To which I shrug and stifle all my negative strangling-type thoughts, which take five minutes to write down. On my way back from brushing my teeth, I see Salminder in his screened-in area, reading beneath twinkling lights.

"Knock, knock," I say, scratching at the screening.

He starts, and I realize he'd been asleep with the book in his lap.

"Sorry, shit, sorry," I say and start to turn. I'm stealing his healing sleep. I'm actively killing the guy.

"No, no." He waves me inside. "Don't swear."

"Sorry."

"Tina's asleep," he says and then adds after a moment, "Sleep has not come easily to either of us these last weeks."

"I'm not helping."

"You lost your grandma," he says. "This whole decision must be difficult."

I sit in a wicker chair that creaks and then we listen to the silence. I may fear the dark, but the best thing about living in the woods is the night sounds. The crickets and owls are my favorites. Coyotes and wolves I can do without, but in my tin can I handle them.

"I'm wasting everyone's time. Everyone's money," I whisper. And I don't say, but think, *Now I'm wasting yours, and you don't have any left.*

"It's an important question to ask yourself," he says finally. "At any age."

"What's the meaning of life?"

"That's the one." Salminder chuckles. "I've found happiness in many, many things. I've lived all over the world. I've done many jobs. But here, I have peace."

We sit and listen to the night for a few minutes, and it's

almost as if he's trying to share what it is he means. He watches me with a soft smile and liquid eyes.

"I need to get out of here. I don't see how my mom and Crystal can do this every summer. I won't find the meaning of life, not here, not in an RV park," I say.

Salminder leans forward. "Do you think a Russian has a better chance of figuring out the meaning of life than an American?"

"No," I say.

"Chinese then?"

I shake my head.

"What about a rich person versus a poor one? Or fat versus thin? Gay or straight? Does one gender have a better chance than another?"

"No, I guess not. Shouldn't."

"What about someone in a prison cell, do you think they could figure it out? On a boat, in space, on a ski hill?" He watches me in silence.

"Okay, okay, I get it."

"So it if it doesn't matter who you are, how rich you are, where you are or what you're doing, then why can't you find your meaning of life here in this very RV park?"

I hesitate.

Salminder has his finger up. "You know, I think the destitute have less of a chance. If you're too hungry to think. Too cold for hope. That would make it more difficult. But that's not you, is it? You have a roof. Food. Family. Friends. The path lies open to you."

I glance around as if I've missed that path, as if I've missed the riches of which he speaks, but Salminder doesn't smile.

"Family? Really?" I laugh. "And friends, I dunno about that either. I never see my buddies from town during the summer. I've got Deneze and Tina, but most my friends are online."

"The lucky kid is the one with one person who believes in them. One. That's all it takes."

"No one thinks I can do this."

"Then you are not listening," he says. "After a while you need to stop making excuses for yourself. Next year won't be different. A different location won't change things. Once you have the roof, food, security, more money changes nothing—if you use it right, it can make life easier, but it won't give you meaning."

"What will then? Can my games?" My hands ache. I'm squeezing them blotchy red and white.

"It's all. *All.* I repeat, all of it is up here." He taps his head in the same way that Dalen had. "And I'm dying, so you have to listen to me."

I almost pull off a smile, but it's too soon to laugh at cancer.

Chapter 23

In my trailer, I wake to Dalen's huge, hovering grin. The chin's purple where my mother hit him. "Who can do it?" he demands.

I shrink beneath my covers and remind myself to lock the trailer door at night.

The covers are yanked off. "You can!" he shouts.

"It's still dark," I cry.

"What an opportunity!"

"You're psycho," I accuse and shudder in the cold.

"Everyone I work with has a list of work to do that's pages long. You told me yours. Sleeping is overrated. Get better quality sleep, less quantity. By sleeping two hours less you gain a quarter more of your productive time. That's ten years of life based on the average lifespan, and we're not average, are we, Ray?"

I've curled up with my knees to my chest, but I nod. "I'm so average. Below average. Above average sleeper."

"There are mystic monks in this world who have never slept. Now up!"

"That doesn't make sense, even monks need to sleep." I

groan. "I'm a teenager, I'm supposed to sleep—lots. I'm losing inches of height here."

"Fatigue is a creation of the mind. I need no sleep. An hour sometimes here and there. But people are wasting years with all this sleep stuff. You get sleepy in class? You do go to school, right?"

"Yeah." *For now.*

"How about at recess? You sleepy then?"

"No."

"See. The problem is that we surround ourselves with tasks that fail to engage us. Make your life a recess and you need never sleep again."

"Tell that to my teachers," I say and cover my head with a pillow.

He flips through my journal. "Good, you . . . uh . . . you have quite a lot here really . . . actually. Not sure anyone has ever filled out so many negative thoughts on their first day . . . ," he trails off and then slams the covers closed. "Not to worry, the trick is to turn negative thoughts into positive ones! That's today's task. Mental alchemy. What happens when we have a negative thought?"

I sigh. He's obviously not about to leave. I flop about on my bed until I am at the edge of the mattress and then I swing my feet to the floor and rest my elbows on my knees, chin in hands.

"Thoughts lead to actions, actions to habit, habit to destiny," he says. "Bad thoughts start like little larvae under your skin, where they grow and mature and then lay a thousand eggs that flow about you until you are nothing more than a host of evil negativity.

"What separates the positive from the negative is how we process stuff up here. Every setback, big or small, is a chance to learn. The glass isn't half-full, or half-empty. It's full. Unless you launch it into space and then I'll give you empty, but even then there are neutrinos that shoot—"

"It's like you're a big motivational poster of a sunrise," I say and push myself out of bed and over to the Kraft Dinner pot. You can tell how dried out it is by the shade of orange. This pot's noodles are dark. I have to scrape through the crunchy top layer to the lighter orange beneath.

Dalen's usually dusky skin color has paled.

"Okay, okay, so you've heard that one about the glass. Did you know that the Chinese word for crisis is written with two characters, one that spells danger and the other opportunity?"

I gag a little on a crunchy bit and then keep chewing.

"There's also some truth to the line you are what you eat, you know?" he says.

"Then I am a stale noodle," I say.

"Aha!" He holds the journal aloft. "That's your next step. What is your mantra?"

"Om?"

"You joke, but 'om' is designed to clear your mind. We'll work on meditation later. Only in silence can we find truth. Om is a good mantra. Tell me, though—do you have a password for your computer? Social media accounts?" I nod. "Is it the same one for them all? Probably, right? What is it?"

I have to take a swig of milk to force the congealed mass of cheesy starch down. "I can't tell you that."

"I'm going to want you to change it anyway."

The noodles reach my stomach, where they join panic-berg. "KDman," I say and flush.

"KD?" He holds up the box of Kraft Dinner. "How many times do you enter KDman a day?"

"About a dozen."

"So, twelve times a day you actually call yourself, in secret, 'KDman'? And then you describe yourself to me as a stale noodle."

"It was a joke."

"What you need to understand is that there are no jokes, that you are what you think you are, what you say you are. Do you know what happens to kids whose parents tell them that they're no good, that they'll never amount to anything?"

My hands tighten around the pot.

"Usually they start believing it." He's dropped his voice to a whisper and stepped in even closer. This is so early for this conversation. "You can trick your brain. Laugh, even fake laugh, and you will be happier. Think positively and your brain will physically begin to change. What would happen if you changed your password to something you actually want yourself to be? What would that be? After we're all done here and you have your million bucks, you have your meaning of life, what will Ray look like? Shut your eyes and tell me. Visualize."

He's waiting, so I try. I imagine the expression on my mom's face when Sam Peregrine says I got the meaning of life correct. "I see myself with everyone who said I couldn't do it crushed beneath me."

"No!" The shout rings out, and in the distance I hear someone yell—*Shut up*! "No. There's nothing good in that. See yourself crushed beneath yourself. That's noble. Try again. Shut your eyes. Who is Better-Ray?"

The little man with the mane of silver seems to fill the entire camper. He's not going anywhere. At least, not until he gets somewhere with me. So I try again. What does a Ray who knows the meaning of life look like? *Better-Ray*. Unbidden I appear in my mind, and I am . . . better. "I'm smiling. Dressed neater and I'm . . . strong."

"Big muscles?" he asks.

"No, but stronger, my eyes are smiling too, and everyone's there, everyone's happy." I'm surprised by this. I thought I'd want to see myself in my own apartment playing games with an even bigger pot of KD—maybe one of the gourmet kinds with chopped hot dogs and extra cheese.

"I've got it. Here's your first new password, are you ready?"

"Shoot."

"Happycamperhappycamp."

"Happy camper . . . ?"

"Happy camp. Think you can handle that?"

I nod. "But I'm not sure Better-Ray lives in a camp. Actually, I know he doesn't."

"Fine, just change your passwords. And at every meal, every time you dig into your orange goo, I want you to visualize your goal. If you can see it, you can be it."

"See it, be it."

"Do this in silence. Silence increases willpower and willpower makes change and change can bring destiny!"

"Destiny? I'm seventeen," I say.

"You're young, but time passes fast. Time is your greatest asset, and you need to think of it as more valuable than money. Because it is." His voice cracks a little, and suddenly he doesn't look like he's performing for a television audience. Thoughts of Salminder intrude on me. "Think like you could be dead tomorrow. What are you going to do today? Focus on those things."

I fold back on to the bed and stare up at the ceiling. Rain patters on the steel roof. "It all sounds so good when you say it, but when you leave, I won't remember anything."

"It takes time, daily work, I can't emphasize practice enough. An athlete won't win a medal without training. Why would you think this would be easy? The reason people don't find their meaning is that they don't work hard enough for it. It's why we use secrets like mantras, but there's a reason I coach for one month. It takes three weeks to form a habit, and once you have a habit, you have . . . ." He looks at me expectantly. "Come on. What comes after habit?"

"Destiny? Really? Here? Running a campground?"

Dalen looks uncertain. "Yes! It's about action, not location, not job. Never has anyone confessed on their deathbed that they wished they had spent more time at the office."

I'm not making the connection. "Like a doctor's office?"

Dalen frowns. "Only if you're a doctor, so no."

"I've never set foot in a real office. Maybe my mom's office, the camp's office, if you count that."

"Do you want to spend time there?"

"No way."

"Then, yes! Count that office! Focus! Unfocused heat does not burn. Find what you truly love and then focus all of your energy toward that."

Dalen's eyes shine. He has that same aura he talked about me getting, like he's larger than life. Some of what he says makes sense, I guess, but it feels like sand running through my fingers.

"I can help you blaze brighter than you ever thought possible," he continues. "But you need to want to change. You told me this wasn't for money or revenge. Tell me how you see yourself. Look in the mirror and tell me."

I step from the kitchen and stare into a cracked floor-to-ceiling mirror. It wasn't cracked before, and I suspect it broke a few days ago when I was holed up gaming.

Licks of brown hair sprout from my head. I haven't had a shower in a few days and mud flakes from the back of my neck. Shirtless, in sweatpants, I don't look strong. I look pasty. Even though I can see my ribs I still have a saggy belly. Red flecks my arms where hot burger grease has splattered and blistered the skin. Bags underscore my eyes and my forehead has blotches of acne. At least the bug bites aren't bad anymore.

I describe myself to him. "Tall, thin, funny, independent."

He lifts an eyebrow. "How do others see you?"

I swallow. "Lazy, loser, aimless, parasitic . . . dork."

"Do you think they're right?"

"No. Yes. Partly."

"Stop lying to yourself. You are not a lazy, aimless loser. You have acted like one. You formed a habit of it, and habits can be broken. What's your mantra?"

"Happycamperhappycamp."

"Good, now go. Any time you think something negative, counter it with a positive. Write it down. A written word is a contract with yourself."

"Okay, Coach," I say.

His lips spread in a wide, toothy grin.

Chapter 24

Happycamperhappycamp.

The journal presses at my thigh.

I searched my floor and couch for some clean and unstained clothing and managed one, but not both. I wear a clean pair of jean shorts with paint spatter and an unstained but moderately malodorous T-shirt with a Dalek on the front. Under it are the words, *You are irrelevant.*

I feel nervous stepping out of my camper. I don't want to face everything. It's not a happy camp. It's not, and *I* am why. To change the world, even my corner of it, is overwhelming.

It's raining.

But not hard enough to keep the bugs back.

Today sucks.

I step back into the trailer out of the rain and write. - *Today sucks.* And then. + *It doesn't have to. Rain is good for plants and water and life itself.*

See, not so hard. Just stupid.

- *This task is stupid* + *Control your thoughts control your destiny.*

- *Bugs* . . . Can't I still hate mosquitoes? They kill more people than wars. + *Dragonflies and some turtles eat mosquito larvae.* I slip the journal into a plastic bag and then lift my arms to the skies as they open up. It's warm, despite it being early. The rain dampens the camp sounds and keeps everyone indoors and not shouting at me. *I'm so positive!* I sense eyes on me and try to remember if Crystal's gone out hunting or not. As my boots slop along the side of the road, a pickup truck roars past, hits a puddle, splashing me.

Why should I bother?

I freeze and slowly turn around. I see him. Dalen. I can't make out his face under the hood of his raincoat, but silver hair cascades down the front. I walk a few steps toward the washrooms and then turn again. He's still there. The same distance away.

"Don't mind me. I won't get in your way. I'm shadowing," Dalen says.

It's creepy, but I continue to the shed. The buckets slop as I put them on the shower floor and then I start at the far side. The floors are muddy. I write in the journal.

- *I hate mud.* + *But others like it. Like pigs and monster truck rally enthusiasts.*

Dalen has taken up sentry at the door.

"You could help," I say as I grab a drooling scrub brush.

"Wouldn't be fair to you," he says. "If I help you now, what would you do when I'm gone?" I roll my eyes. "As you work, listen to the sounds, smell the detergent, think about the feel of the brush. Regain control of your thoughts and be present."

On my knees I begin to scour the tiles, and I think of all the things I could be doing that would be more fun if only he'd help me finish. After a minute of brushing and dipping the brush back in the pail, Dalen says, "As you work, clear your mind. I've heard a rhythm. Shooka-shooka-shooka-splash. Three scrubs, and then a pail dip. Work it."

I sigh at the floor, silently wishing he'd disappear.

Shooka-shooka-splash. Shooka-splash.

I roll my eyes and try again. Shooka-shooka . . .

I don't think I manage more than two shookas before some stray thought intrudes, but it's not until I'm wiping down the bathroom mirrors that he pipes up again.

"In each mirror, picture Better-Ray. Visualize. See it, be it."

- I hate having Yoda as my shadow. + Yoda dies.

I try to picture myself as I had in the trailer, but the more I scrub, the more I clean, the harder it becomes, and I'm stuck with Dorky-Ray.

"If you can see it, you can—"

I hold up my hand to interrupt him, and write in my journal.

- If he says See-it be-it again, I will kill him and go to jail. + I wouldn't have to hear those words another time.

"Go," I say, trying to think of something that will make him leave. "I . . . I'm really feeling this. I really think I'll get it if I'm alone for a bit. Silence, right?"

"See it, be it," he repeats as he leaves. I shake a fist at his back.

The washroom takes another couple of hours. By the time I'm done, the heavy clouds have brightened and the smell of burning steak's on the wind despite the rain. It's ten, the earliest I've finished with cleaning since I took over. The ruts are beginning to fill with water, and I try to decide what I should do next. I look from the ruts to the steam smoking from the lid of

Obelix's barbecue. If we had a truck rally, I wouldn't have to bother filling the ruts for a few days . . .

I laugh at that, imagining the trucks ripping around the park. I head for the pool and stop. *Why not?* The roads can't get any worse.

"Steak and coffee, have them for breakfast and you'll always have a good day," Obelix says as I near.

"You ever run a truck rally?" I ask.

"No," he replies and takes a drink of coffee from a black mug. "Do you want to try?"

He pauses with the tongs. "You offering me a job?"

"Not like a paid job or anything," I say. "More of a volunteer position. It's supposed to rain for a few days. We'll have lots of mud, and I saw how disappointed you were."

I'm looking down the whole time, beginning to wonder if this was such a good idea after all. Who the heck wants to organize something for nothing? But when I glance back up, he rushes to clutch my head into his hairy chest.

"Yes!" he cries. "Of course." I pry his meaty forearm from my cheek and wipe my face with palms smelling of bleach. Woken by his exclamation, his little dog's yipping away at my ankles. "Shush, Ideafix." And I smile. "I have to get going then, don't I?" He shoves me away as if I'm slowing him down. "Take advantage of the rain. Three days—no, I need time—six days from now. The first annual Sunny Days—Mudslinger—no, we need a name— something catchy, Muddy Days? No. Do we charge?" That last bit is directed at me.

I hadn't thought of that. "No, let's keep it small, but everyone has to agree to make the road flat again after. The whole park."

"Every tire track filled. That makes sense. I see what you're after, Swami."

For a second I glance over my shoulder, expecting to see Dalen there, but he's not. Obelix is talking to me.

I practically skip over to one of the rental trailers; a miner's checking out, says there's too much mold and she's moving. By the time I reach it, she's already packed up.

"Should be condemned, kid." She tosses me the key. She wears a beaten cowboy hat and a long oilskin. "Black mold eating through the steel."

"All the rain," I say, and she shakes her head.

"Not the rain, not the rain."

With a tip of her hat she slams the door to her pickup and slides onto the road. The camper trailer is from the forties or thereabouts, probably back from when my grandma opened the place. There's five of them in a row, all one-bedroom jobs like mine, but they have a certain nostalgia to them. In each window hangs an old dream catcher. Signatures from campers cover the exterior. I set the buckets down beside the door and climb into the trailer to check it out. A dingy bulb casts pallid light over lime green walls.

I smell the earthy damp and hear the drips before I see the rivulets in the corners. Mold has left a signature of its own. Water runs inside, following a funnel of creeping black. Aside from the mold, the woman left the place fairly clean. The cushions even feature fresh lengths of duct tape where their vinyl had torn. I still need to wipe everything down and empty the trash. I scrub at the mold, taking off a top layer, but it's chewed into the metal.

Fifteen minutes later I'm outside inspecting where the water's getting in. I've pulled the picnic table over and stand on the top to check out the corners of the trailer. Rain rattles from the rooftop. The signatures are up here too.

Martha – 1967 – This place is the best. So long and thanks for the pie.

Catherine – 1972 – You saved my life.

JoJo – Summer 1968 – Coming here is coming home, I'd forgotten that life can hold more than pain. And the pie!

This is not the sort of graffiti I'd expected. Not the "I was here' stuff on most the walls. These are messages of gratitude. But they couldn't have been meant for here. Not this campground. Not for Grandma. I chuckle and run my fingers along the leaking seam in the metal.

Anna-Marie – 1977 – There's a special place for those who give more than they get.

Trevor and Lisa – 1965 – Sunny Days lit up our hearts and filled our stomachs.

I blink and hop down from the table. Written over a bunch of other fading notes I read, *Bob – 2017 – Good riddance, at least I didn't contract a disease.* And another: *Mosquito – 2015 – Thank you for this special bug-infested haven.*

That's more like what I've come to expect. Not a mention of pie.

The trailer seams need something like a tar, but for now I return with duct tape and patch it up, knowing that I don't really plan on ever sealing it properly. Workers up here have few options, so the trailer will be rented by tomorrow, leaky or not.

I swing the empty buckets on my way to drop them off when pigtailed girl runs up alongside. In the distance I watch as Dalen does chin-ups using the rusty swing set. He's like a robot. I swear he does a couple with only one arm.

"Hi, Mr. Ray." She smiles big. "Is the iceberg melted?" For a second I look inside to my stomach, but panic-berg's still there.

"Almost," I say. "Maybe tomorrow. Did you know an iceberg sank the Titanic? They can be huge and dangerous."

A tiny furrow appears between her eyebrows. I wondered when those wrinkles start, and here I am seeing this one begin. If all it takes for a kid to be successful is one person to believe in them, then maybe all it takes is one person for a kid to distrust, to start the brow wrinkle.

"My mommy said tomorrow means one more sleep. It's been . . ." She starts counting on her fingers and runs out.

"Yeah, I know. Not everyone's tomorrow's the same. But this time it's one more sleep."

She smiles again, but I see that the furrow's still there. And I know where they come from. Broken promises.

Chapter 25

Pulled Beef's quiet. Earlier I heard Tina crying inside, but I gave her some space. Privacy. When I go for my shift, the place is immaculately clean, the counter a mirror, the grill greaseless and the floor as scrubbed as, well . . . there's only so much you can do for stained and curled linoleum tile.

Tina sits on the floor, thumbing through Dalen's books. I'd left them scattered there. "What do you think?" she asks. "Think any of this is going to work?"

I pause, about to complain about Dalen, and then stop myself. Her eyes are puffy from crying. "How's your dad? How are you?"

She shrugs. "Trying to keep busy. Don't want to think about it."

We don't have many customers. Rain falls in a steady sheet, and the only people who come drive up, shouting for a burger from their trucks. It's not busy, so she cleaned instead. "Maybe I should leave you in charge of the camp?" I say.

"Maybe," she agrees. "You can focus on figuring out the meaning of life. I'd sure like to know." A scrap of paper rests as a bookmark between the pages.

We sit listening to the rain. A truck drives past but doesn't stop.

"Do you think I can figure out the meaning of life?" I ask.

"I think you can do anything you want."

There's no humor in her eyes. Part of her reply sounded like an accusation, as if I can, but she can't.

"That's part of the problem though, isn't it. That we can do anything."

"Not like brain surgeon's an option." She laughs, but not cruelly. Not *really* cruelly.

"Why not? If I work really hard in high school this year, I could graduate with a scholarship to university." I don't mind her laughing even if it's at my expense, not if it makes her feel better. "I'm not saying it for sure would happen, but it could."

"You've got too many choices. Poor you."

"It's paralyzing. When I'm gaming, I don't think about this stuff."

"Only with me. Lucky me."

Tina's angry. I fight the urge to bite back. I struggle for something positive to say. "You make me want to try." And that's way too much. I'm shocked at what just came out my mouth.

She bites her lip, and her eyes shimmer. Then she slams the covers of the book together. "That's nice," she says. "I gotta go. Dad had another appointment today. Setting up for another line of treatment."

"Good luck," I say, and she uses my shoulder to pull herself up. My first thought is, she touched me again. I know I could interpret that as my being a table or something, but I don't. A band of steel wraps itself around my lungs and doesn't let up squeezing until she's gone. For a while I listen to rain patter on the tin roof.

Finally, I push up off the floor, crank up the grill, and start on a Ray Special, frying the onions and garlic before layering in mayo, relish, hot sauce, everything. Then I scoop the mess into a bowl.

Someone honks.

"Two burgs!" comes a yell through the crack in a truck window, then the crack closes.

I draw a breath. Tina partially cooked a half dozen burgers already, so while they heat I focus on the toppings.

"What do you want on them?" I call out to the truck. But their glass is a blur of rain. Music thumps, jostling the rain on the truck hood and roof. *You deserve a bun with some mustard,* I think. More stuff to write down. What's the positive? But before I can think of something they honk again.

Fine then. They're getting Ray's Special. I divide the goo between two burgers and tuck everything together and wrap it tight in silver foil.

I hesitate and consider making them proper burgers, but then the truck honks a third time. More negative thoughts . . . I grab the burgers I've prepared, dash out, and slip them through the narrow opening. Greedy hands take them and then drop out a ten-dollar bill. The window closes even before I have a chance to say thank you.

Back at the grill I make my own Ray Special. I use the same recipe, but this time I add fresh lettuce, tomato, onion, pickles, cheese. The cheese I layer on the patties once they're flipped. By the time the goo is ready, the cheese has bubbled, and I toast the bun in a bit of butter. The only thing missing is bacon, but when I bite into it, I know I'm eating the best burger Pulled Beef has ever produced.

Five minutes later another truck pulls up.

"Swami!" the jack shouts. "Give me one of the new fancy ones."

It's a second before I understand. The Ray Special. They're calling for it.

I comply, but add in all the new elements. Within the hour I've had three more requests for a "Swami Burger."

A third truck pulls up behind two others. Its driver approaches in an oilskin coat. Everyone's doors open then, and a line forms in pouring rain to ensure they keep their spot.

For what should have been a quiet day because of the rain, it grows busier quickly, as word spreads of the Swami Burger.

I know it's not the meaning of life. It's not brain surgery and I didn't mean for it to happen. It's just a really yummy hamburger. But one step at a time. *Happycamperhappycamp.*

Chapter 26

It's 5:00 a.m. Dalen's banging on my door. I know it's him because he has a distinct knock, like automatic machine gun fire. *Rat-ta-ta-ta-ta-ta-tat. Rat-ta-ta-ta-ta-ta-tat.*

I throw open the door and then collapse back into my bed.

"Part of the meaning of life is not wasting it," he says.

I smell the coffee on him. It infuses him. He flips pages in the journal I left beside my computer—I gamed for an hour last night and learned I lost four followers. I can no longer say I have "dozens."

"Good, good, yes, yes," he whispers as he reads. "Yes! When you open yourself to positive thoughts, you change not only your life but those around you. Like this Obelix fellow. It was a good day, wasn't it? Who is this Tina character? What made you say something nice, when you wanted to get angry at her?"

"Her dad's got cancer," I mutter.

"Good!"

I sit up and glare at him. "How is that *good*?"

"Not good that he's sick. Good that you treated her well. You saw things from her side."

"Well, it's sad." I slump.

"You don't think anyone else in this camp has a sad story?"

Not a night goes by that I don't hear someone cursing or crying or screaming. Campers are like fishbowls—there are no secrets here. "Probably."

"But you don't know, right?" Dalen sits down on my bed. "Let me tell you. In this camp, someone's father is dying. Someone's mother recently died. A woman has fled an abusive husband with her daughter in tow. Another camper comes here because it's too far for him to drive out for alcohol so, unable to drink, he dries out every summer, and another is here because he's lonely and people in camp talk to him. He feels like he's not invisible here—his hobby is shadow puppets, pretty good at it too. You learn these things when you don't need to sleep. Can you tell me the names that match the stories?"

"Tina, my mom, the little girl and her mother . . . I can guess the last one, but I've never seen him." *Light show, dude.* Now I feel badly about my note on his door asking him to hood his lights. *Stop all your loud shadow puppetry!* "I don't know the rest."

"Nor need you to. You should treat everyone as though they've lost a loved one."

This is all pretty morbid. I say, "Live like you're dying, treat everyone as if someone just died. Weee . . . What happened to 'happycamperhappycamp'?"

"That's for you to teach yourself. This is for how you change the way you treat others. Got it?"

I nod. "But how is that going to teach me the meaning of life?"

I asked the right question, because he leaps up on the bed and points down at me.

"What's your goal for today?"

I want to say climb Big Mountain, but for some reason that doesn't seem as important any more. I'm annoyed that I've lost followers, followers that took so long to garner, but that won't help with happycamperhappycamp. The thought of the pigtailed girl and her mother using this as a place of refuge hit home. It sent warm flushes of shame through me.

"I'm going to fix the pool. Get it open. And be on time for my Pulled Beef shift."

Dalen grins.

"Are you opening the pool because it's part of your job?"

I frown. "Well, yeah, but . . ."

"It's more than that," he says—he knows.

"The girl wants to swim."

"You're treating her like she needs help, and she does. What's more, she looks up to you and you've broken your promises to her. When we keep to our goals, we keep promises to ourselves and others. When we keep promises, we believe in our goals and can achieve them. This is why we start small. So that when we know the meaning of life, we see it as something achievable and not another promise we intend to break." He drops the journal back on my chest and points at my climbing rope. "That rope is strong because it is made with many thin threads. Your meaning will be strong because it will be the culmination of many smaller goals. Keep with the thought journaling, but Ray, the meaning of life is most likely not a yummy hamburger. Nor is it found on a mountain top, not for most of us."

I press my palms into the hollows of my eyes. I want to hold them there; it's soothing to be blind. "I'd rather be playing video games."

Dalen tugs my wrists, dragging me up and onto my feet. "Have you heard of interactive virtual reality? You know, where you can enter a digital world in which you can influence what is around you? You can make the flowers grow to the size of plates. The rain fall sideways."

"Yeah, I guess. But the technology isn't quite there yet."

"What if I told you it is there. You don't even need any special technology to see it."

"I'd say giddyup and that I don't believe you." This is a trick; I can smell it.

"Look out your window. Try to think of everything with a negative mindset. As if everything's going wrong and will go wrong and everyone's against you. What do you see?"

I have to open the window to see through it.

"Mud, jobs, my hands hurt at the thought of everything I need to do. How everyone here seems sick with some cough, how they're killing themselves with cigarettes and I have to breathe it in as I walk by. The trailer park's a prison." I blink. That wasn't very hard and a little too real. I shiver and rub the gooseflesh from my arms.

"Okay, now let's see how you do with a positive view. What do you see? Everything is beautiful. Life is a gift. Helping people's a calling, and not a chore."

I'm nodding, but I still see all the work even though I can't say that. I shut my eyes, picture Tina—a smirking Tina—and then reopen them.

"There's a flower over there." I point at the red flanges of a late tulip, struggling through the thick grasses. "And . . . I wonder if we should have smoking areas of the camp, and non-smoking areas. And . . . I'm getting these calluses on my hands and they're actually sort of cool."

Dalen's clapping. A slow clap, but still.

"Did you see the flower the first time you looked?"

I shake my head.

"The real world is a construct of our perceptions. If you don't see the flower, it might as well not even be there. Change your perception, change the world."

My shoulders sag as I struggle to control my thoughts.

"It was harder to think positively, wasn't it?" he asks.

"Way harder."

"That's because it's not a habit. Negative thoughts come easy because that's what you're used to thinking, but this is *your* interactive virtual reality, it is what *you* make of it."

I get it. The flowers. Opportunities to challenge the negative. It's not the sort of virtual reality I'd hoped for, like fighting monsters with flaming swords, but . . .

My fingers catch in my tangled curls. I turn on the hot plate and sit a pot of water on it. The crate of Kraft Dinner should have had a dozen boxes left, but it's empty. "Wha—"

Dalen drops a bag of rabbit food on the table. "Oatmeal," he says. "Breakfast of champions."

"You can't take my food."

"You're paying me one hundred thousand dollars. The least I can do is provide a proper breakfast."

"I don't want a proper breakfast. That's not breakfast. It's missing three food groups: sugar, ketchup, and cheese."

"Those aren't food groups."

"Taste groups then."

"Didn't you once have scurvy?"

"How do you know *everything*?"

"This is only the beginning," Dalen says, and I can't tell if it's a promise, or a threat.

Chapter 27

After Dalen leaves, I stare for a minute at the oatmeal, shake my head, and start the chores. I'm already halfway through the women's bathroom when he catches back up with me.

"A good breakfast is a mission accomplished," he says. "Don't fail with your first mission of the day."

Shooka-shooka-shooka-splash. I pretend to be meditating. He's right. I am hungry, but I'm also energized.

Shook-shook-shook-shook-dip. Shooka-shook-shook-splash.

"Ray, it has to be consistent. Like 'om.'"

I pause with my hand on the brush, wishing he'd disappear, and then I try again.

Shooka-shooka-shooka-splash.

I sense his smiling.

In the mirror, I search for Better-Ray and then go back to the floor.

I rip through the cleaning of the washroom. For a couple of moments in the men's washroom, I swear my mind goes blank and there is nothing in it—and not in a dork way—in a way that opens me up to the scents, the polished tile, the echoes of my cleaning, and the ache of my knees.

Dalen winks at me. He knows. "Imagine a life where all moments were like that. How alive you'd feel," he says.

Scraping goo from the shower ceiling, I don't even gag. It's as though I'm on autopilot and separate from my mind. When I finish, Dalen's gone. Campfires winkle in the early morning and wood smoke melts the gut-berg a bit—a bit. The mud's phenomenal. With the steady rains, ruts brim with milky puddles as deep as my knee.

Dark gray skies hang low. The morning feels longer as I stand beside the pool. The berg floats, still and stubborn in the center. Two bergs really, a smaller one that has fused to the larger, both wreathed in a crown of leaves. I scrape the leaves from the surface but I'm wasting time. In two hours my shift at Pulled Beef starts, a double shift so that Tina can be with Salminder for his new treatment. I promise myself that I won't be late.

I brought a shovel with me and fight a sudden urge to start filling ruts. I see the ruts for what they are. They're a waste, an excuse to break my promises. I realize I've been making these excuses for some time now. I hook the top of the berg with the leaf skimmer, and slowly, ever so slowly, like a freighter turning at sea, the berg inches toward me. The ice crunches as it reaches the side, removing a strip of greenish-yellow algae from the liner. The shovel pierces the bridge between the two bergs, and the smaller bit bobs free. This piece is one-twentieth the size of the larger and, even so, it takes all my strength to roll it out of the pool. My arms are soaked, hands frozen and pants drenched. Sharp angles of ice have scraped my forearms. But a small goal's been achieved.

With the shovel, I jab the remaining berg. The pointed shovel tip skips off, leaving only a white nick. I jab again, and another chip flies. This method might work if I had all week. I reach into the frigid water, find a lip of ice to grab and haul. The berg floats up an inch and then settles back down when I release. What can I do? It's still too big. I have to let it melt. It'll be another few days at least.

I turn around. There at the fence, fingers threaded through the chain link, stands the little girl. Her eyes are big and not even looking at me; they're on the pool. What kind of hell has she fled from? She's used to disappointment—that I can tell. Those wrinkles at her brow are not from me, not only from me, but also from scrunching her face in fear.

I kick off my muddy shoes and pull my shirt over my head. This will hurt. I don't think it'll work, but at least I'll have showed her that I tried.

There's a tradition in some places where they jump into water through an ice hole. To be honest, I always felt that to be stupid. They call it the "polar bear dip" because only polar bears would enjoy something like that. But no one has ever accused me of being smart. I hesitate with my toes over the pool edge.

"Go on," the little girl calls through the chain link.

I brush the water with my foot. This was a mistake. Jumping into cold water is not something you do slowly.

"Just jump," she says. "What's stopping you?"

"Quit talking to Dalen." I swing my arms and jump. My lungs collapse. My heart stops. My brain blanks. It's pain. It's stupid. And then it's as if an electrical current runs through me because my lungs, my heart, and my brain surge back into action at a billion times their normal rates. I shout in short tortured gasps. A tiny fraction of my thoughts is devoted to the reason why I made the leap. Or perhaps it's just the glee of a certain little girl I make out through the blood screaming in my ears.

I claw and sputter at the pool-berg, ice cutting at my palms. I get low, ducking beneath the surface, and shoulder it. It only floats into deeper water. I still can't catch my breath, but the initial panic's gone. I manage shallow pants that keep the encroaching fringe of darkness at bay. I slowly begin to . . . warm. It's the strangest feeling, but the longer I stay, the more deadened my limbs go, the warmer the sensation.

Which, of course, means I'm probably dying.

I glance at the girl; she's clapping. I gasp another breath. And I know I have to do this.

I dive down and swim below the blurred edge of the berg. It's big with great divots where some parts of the ice have melted faster than others. My lungs begin to spasm even as warmth floods me, and the darkness creeps tighter. Something hard presses at the base of my skull.

Crouched beneath the ice, I push up on the berg with my palms. Ice rises, and the higher it goes, the more it weighs. It's not far enough out of the water for me to heave it out. I ease it back down and, neck bent, rest the burning ice on my back and push again. The frigid muscles in my thighs twang with the effort. A sense of peace settles over me. As the darkness closes in, I give up and breaststroke for the surface.

I reach air and wheeze. My hands are clubby with cold and bounce off the pool ledge. A hard thing knifes into my head— the worst brain freeze ever. I climb the slimy bottom to a shallower area, until I'm out of the water to my waist. Body red with cold, goose fleshed and shuddering.

I roll onto the pool side and rub blood back into my limbs. The pain in my head subsides.

"Sorry," I chatter.

The girl gives me a wry smile.

"It's too heavy," she says. "You need help."

Chapter 28

I lie on the edge of the pool for a few minutes, letting a brief pocket of sun warm me.

"Don't be afraid of failure." I open my eyes. Dalen leans over the fence. "Every event has a lesson. They are essential. Have you cheated? Done something you're ashamed of, like a hit and run?"

"What? No," I say. "Have you?"

He flushes before adding, "You'll never be remembered for how many times you fell down, only for the one time that you didn't."

"You going to help me?" I ask.

"I'm not here for long, Ray, not long," he replies and walks away.

I shut my eyes again. The sun's baking. It sends prickling fire through my limbs. All I want to do is drift off to sleep.

"So you getting up, or what?" the little girl asks.

I sigh and sit forward. The clouds have rushed back in. "Okay," I say. "Give me a bit."

Her neck bends so far forward, it's like it's broken. She starts away.

"I'll be back," I say, but she doesn't turn around as I head to my trailer. I need a new plan.

On YouTube I watch an explanation of pulley systems and generally bone up on some physics. I don't have any pulleys, but I do have the climbing carabiners and rope; maybe they'll come in handy after all. If I hook them to two points on the fence, I will have a pulley system. The only trouble is how to attach it all to the pool-berg.

I have rope, two carabiners, one strap, and a determination to prove to myself that I can do this.

Back at the pool, the girl's eating a bag of chips and drinking from a can of Coke. "Is it cold?" she asks.

"Yes," I say.

"Are you going to get the ice out?" she asks.

"Yes," I say.

"My mom says you should just turn the heat on in the pool."

"If only the pool had a heater," I say. The girl squints and I hold up my hands. "It's a good idea. But this pool is heated by the sun." She crunches on a chip. "And summer, you know, warmth in general does it," I add. "But it's been cold at night."

She hunts in the foil bag. "I'm watching."

I thread the rope through the carabiners on the fence and then eye the cold water again. I'm dry, in warm clothes, but I know what I have to do. Knowing what to expect makes it worse, but I have to get the strap around the center of the berg or risk having it slip out. I hold one end with the other tied to the loop of rope and jump. The air in my lungs forces its way out, but I manage to keep half and swim under the berg to toss the strap over to the far side.

"I got it!" comes the shout and I hop out to see the little girl, all of forty pounds, struggling to hold the strap, while reaching out over the water on tippy-toes.

"Hey, careful," I say, but it's too late. She's overbalanced on her flipflops and topples into the water. She slips beneath the surface. The iceberg shifts to grind against the pool side. Her body is a blur beneath the ice.

I don't think. I dive, scrape my chin on the bottom, and hammer my shoulder into the berg. In the haze of water, the girl claws at the ice until the iceberg moves. She shoves off the bottom to gasp for air at the wall.

Tears well in her eyes, and she grips the side.

"You okay?" I ask.

She gives these tiny nods. "I hate the iceberg."

I glance back. The strap's still hanging over the middle.

"What d'you say we get it out of here?"

Her smile warms me more than the sun as I haul her out.

"What's your name?" I ask.

"Penny."

"Well, thanks, Penny. I couldn't have got the strap around it without you."

She beams.

I'm careful to keep the strap taut as I knot the ends together and hook on a third carabiner, which I snap to the loop of rope. "Can you pull on that end?" I motion to the end of the rope, which she pulls on until the whole system is tight. I join her. "Hey, you're really good at this. Ready to help me get it out?"

If she nods her head any faster, it's going to fly off.

By pulling on one end of the rope, the mass of the berg is

now distributed between the two carabiners, cutting the weight in half.

She grips the rope behind me. "On three," I say.

She shrieks, "One-two-three!"

I dig my heels in and lean back as the berg slides to the side of the pool and then begins to angle up. But our combined weight and strength isn't enough. The berg settles back in the water.

Penny doesn't seem disheartened. If anything, her smile has broadened. "Now what?" she asks.

I spot the fence post. "I know," I say, and I hook the rope around the post, cutting the weight of the berg into thirds. "Again."

"One-two-three," she says, and we heave.

When the ice rises as far as we can get it, I tighten the loop on the post so that the berg can't slip back into the water. Then we heave again. Bit by bit, the berg lifts from the pool depths. Patterns of pocks are revealed as we unearth it, but even with the clouds, all I can think of is what a beautiful shade of blue. With a sudden release, the ice crunches onto the pool deck.

"We did it!" Penny screams. "We did it!"

I laugh as Penny dances, drenched and with hair plastered to her forehead and cheeks. It feels great. This must be how the meaning of life feels.

It's as fleeting as a dream.

Chapter 29

I arrive late for shift, but I spring up to the counter and smile. I'm fifty-fifty on promises for the day, which is a hundred percent better than usual. On the menu board are now written two items. Burger and Swami Burger. The Swami Burger costs two dollars more. Tina doesn't look over—she's chopping something.

"You said you'd be here," Tina accuses before I open the door.

"Once I started on the pool I couldn't stop," I say. "The little girl—Penny was there and—"

"You're blaming a little girl?" Tina asks.

"No, but—"

"I couldn't go," Tina says. "To my dad's treatment."

I made her miss her dad's cancer treatment.

"No, really?" I say. "You could have kept Pulled Beef closed. People would have understood." But of course Salminder doesn't want anyone to know. Yet, at this point, if I know and Dalen knows, I'm wondering who doesn't know. "You can almost see the pool from here, you could have just yelled."

"You're blaming me?" she asks.

Her lip curls in where she's biting it. The knife slowly slices a tomato. The bin is already overflowing. In the distance, I hear a chainsaw run. I wonder what my mother's up to.

"I can borrow a car, drive you in," I say.

"And this new Swami Burger, it takes twice as long to make. Dad says you were losing money with every one of them you sold yesterday."

I hesitate, not sure how we got on to Swami Burgers. "Salminder wanted you to stay because I was losing him money?" I try to understand.

"No," she says and then slams the knife down so that the tomato splits, pulp spurting over the cutting board. "He doesn't want *me* there."

"Oh," I say. "Then . . . you didn't need me on time."

"What?" Her eyes widen.

"Just saying, because I thought my being late had made it so you couldn't go, and I think you wanted me to feel that way."

"You're not a dork, you're a jerk," she says.

Tears pool at the corner of her eyes, and her hands ball into fists.

"Sorry," I whisper. "I'm sorry I was late. And I'm sorry you couldn't go with your dad."

Her fists unfurl, and I take her hands into mine.

"Didn't want me to come. Said someone has to take care of you." She looks up to the ceiling, chin jutted.

"Wow, he's really pushing me into your arms," I joke. "I'm not sure how comfortable I am with that."

She cocks her head and is straight-faced for a moment and then turns back to the chopping table, shaking her hands free from mine. "Yeah, right." But I caught the smirk.

"I am sorry, Tina. It must be hard for him, too."

She nods as she weeps and my heart breaks a little because I'm making her do it, but she hurts and there's nothing I can do to fix that pain.

The grill ignites, and soon the sounds and smells of sizzling burgers overwhelm her sniffles and even the chainsaw. Blue smoke pumps from near the pool. Even with the pool-berg out, the pool will take a few days to warm enough for swimming. Between now and then, I'll clean the sides and start the pump circulating.

"One burger and one Swami Raymond fortune." I turn at the voice. I know the sarcasm all too well.

"Mother," I reply.

"I see the ruts are still ruts." She glowers, smelling of oil and gasoline.

"Fixing them this week," I say, "All of them after the rain's done."

"Won't write a check for a grader, not while you have two arms and a shovel," she says.

"Not using a grader," I reply.

She eyes me as if searching for something else to accuse me of. "Crystal's off after that grandma-killer again," she says. "The bear. Says it's hanging around. I think she's gone crazy."

I make a show of looking up at the dark sky. "How's the suntan coming?"

"Bad for the skin," she says. "Listen . . . uh." She sighs. "I'm willing to go back to the way it was. I'll do the office work, Crystal can do the cleaning."

"Why would you do that?" I ask.

159

She's looking everywhere except at me.

"I hate the phone ringing and having to write down messages for you. How's that sound? Back to normal." She glances down at her hands. They look like they're wrestling one another.

Tina's stopped chopping.

"Sounds like you want me to give up," I say. I can still hear her and Crystal's laughter.

"Not saying so. I'm just saying I'm willing to help out . . . a bit. So? What d'you say?"

I glance at Tina, who gives me an encouraging nod. I'm not so easily fooled. What's my mom up to?

Today I fulfilled a major stepping stone. I removed the berg. I did all the chores except the office chores and then some. I'm on track. Happy Camper Happy Camp.

"No, I don't think so," I say.

My mom peers at me. "Why the heck not?"

"Yeah, why not?" Tina asks.

"No one thought I could do it. I'm going to prove I can." *And I don't trust you.*

"Fine . . . I believe you, then." The admission comes through clenched teeth. "That better?"

I shrug.

"Can't you see your mama's bored?" Tina says. "Crystal's gone, there's nothing for her to do."

The tips of my mother's ears go bright red.

But if she's bored, it's her fault. I wonder now if taking away the camp will also take away the tools I need to figure everything out.

"You need a hobby," I say.

"There's only so many blocks of ice around, Swami Ray." My mom walks, head down and burger-less, back toward her trailer.

Tina gives me a look that says *oh-come-on*, but I'm not having it. This is my show now. Control your thoughts. Control your actions. Etcetera. *Destiny.*

Later that day, on the way to set up the bonfire, I pass the pool. Someone's turned the pool-berg into a rough-cut bear and the small bergy bit into what could be two bear cubs.

Chapter 30

Five days remain until "Mud and Fire," the name Obelix and I settled on for the truck rally. Mud races for pickup trucks and ATVs. I decided it was time to push my uncle, too, so Obelix is in charge of Mud and Uncle Jamie the Fire. I gave him the same nudge the death of my grandma has given me. When I asked him, he didn't hesitate, just a single glance back to Grandma's statue and then a swift nod, before disappearing as he counted on his fingers.

My days are full. Now that I've told my mom I don't want her help, I've locked myself into getting everything done myself and doing it well enough that she doesn't have a reason to criticize. Every time I catch Tina, she's reading from another of Dalen's books, scribbling on the note that acts as the bookmark. Sometimes I wonder if she should be the one working with Dalen and not me. She's smart. Motivated.

She could use a hand, too.

Every morning, Dalen treats me to oatmeal and has taken to leaving me a prepared salad for lunch. After a weird pep talk about something or other, we go through a session of meditation and visualization of Better-Ray, and then he helps me set my goal for the day. Today, it's to enlist someone. The goal for the week is to enlist the rest of the campers to improve the camp. The pool-berg, for example—that could have happened a lot earlier if I'd had some help.

"If life really is virtual reality, then we might as well make it good," Dalen says as I'm lugging the cleaning fluid and buckets back to the shed. "You have a role in the relationships around you. Don't blame them for anything and don't blame yourself. Accept conflict as something that just is and do better."

"What are you talking about?" Sometimes he runs on as if I understand the stuff he says.

"Remember that you are an animal. You have instincts." He pounds his chest. "These instincts are to survive."

"Sounds smart to me," I say and close the hasp on the shed lock. I had a really good *shooka-shooka-shooka* morning. The forest glows with vibrant greens.

"Not really," Dalen says. "Some of our instincts are obsolete and cause suffering. Most of us have all we need, but instinct is powerful. It pits us against one another. It pushes us to want more and more. To think of the future, at the sacrifice of the present. So say you do get the million dollars. I know that you'll want more."

I snort.

"No, really, I've seen it. A person with one million wants another. A person with half a billion won't be happy until they have another hundred million, or more."

"Okay, so I'm an animal."

"Yes, and you must override these instincts because

everywhere people will use them against you. They will steal your money by marketing to those instincts. Marketers know you are hard-wired to find a mate, to earn money, to carve out a place in the pack to survive. That's not the meaning of life. That's survival, and most of us get caught up in that. Even the richest, even the happily married. They make themselves unhappy by thinking they need more, that another mate might be a little bit better. But when you recognize your instincts, you can head them off."

"What does that mean for happycamperhappycamp?"

"It means finding a higher meaning than survival, and that is helping the pack thrive, not just yourself within it. It means being grateful and being present. It means you need a new password."

"Iamarecruitmentofficer," I say. I'm joking but he fist-bumps me anyways.

I think about what Dalen said after we part. It isn't until I notice Obelix strutting around camp with his pants pulled up to his nipples and his little yipping dog that I understand. For the first time in days, I have a free hour on my hands before my Pulled Beef shift.

I start at trailer site number one. I have a list of everyone in the camp and their assigned site number. This one is Buck Hawley's. He comes to the door of his trailer wearing a black T-shirt stretched over a tight frame. He smells of sawdust and tobacco smoke. I don't know how he makes it through the doorframe without turning sideways.

"Yep," he says, looking down at my clipboard and then back up.

Ropes of tattoos are nearly lost over the dark skin of his arms.

"Hi, Mr. Hawley," I say. "My name's Ray, and I'm in charge of the camp."

For a second time his eyes run over me, and then he leans out of the trailer to look around.

"This a joke?" he asks.

"No, sir, I'm offering fortunes and asking what people want for their camp. How can I make Sunny Days better?"

"Fortunes?"

It had sounded like a fun icebreaker. I'd written a good dozen down that I could use depending on how I read their mood.

"Yeah, I see . . . I see . . ." I wave my arms in a mystical way. He shuts the door.

"How would you like to improve the camp?" I shout.

The trailer stops creaking, which likely means he's stopped moving in it.

"Quieter for the night shifters," he says through the screen. The undercarriage creaks again.

It's wishful thinking but I write the request down. "I see sleep in your future!"

Then I move on to slab two, but Wendy Wilson's out, as is the occupant of slab three, which gives me an idea. Slab one is near to the playground and pool, not ideal if you're on night shift and want to sleep during the day. I only need to find someone who would prefer Buck's site to theirs. Slab four is occupied by a wiry thin woman, with steely hair. She's hanging her washing.

"Hi . . ." I look down at my sheet. "Salema . . ."

"Don't worry, no one can pronounce my last name, what can I do you for?" She keeps pinning up a sheet. A sign at the corner of her slab says, "I'm the bitch with the hitch."

"Well, I was wondering what I can do to help you?"

She smiles. "Like my washing?"

"Uh, more like camp stuff. Anything bug you? Stuff you'd like to change?"

"Sore back. I'd like a good ten years of life back." I make like I'm writing all of this down and she chuckles. "Maybe something social, you know, all the men here hunker in their trailers or their trucks. It's not healthy."

"Yoga, maybe."

We're both laughing.

"I'd pay to see that," she says.

I'm still smiling as I approach the next slab with someone home. It's the mother of the little girl, Penny. When I say hello, she jumps a foot and holds her hand against her chest.

"Sorry," I say. "Didn't mean to frighten you."

She gives a jittery nod and goes back to fiddling with the camping stove, trying to screw on a new fuel canister. Her hand shakes.

"Pool ready?" she mutters.

"Soon," I say.

She scoffs.

Behind her back, I bridle. I stand a little taller, and I squint at her. She checks over her shoulder, catching my look, and hustles around the picnic table as if to put it between us.

I flush with shame. "Sorry," I say. "I'm sorry about the pool. I should have got to it earlier. We don't have many kids— Sorry. Just. I'm sorry. Can I . . ."

What can I do for someone who fled from an abusive

husband? She's wearing the same tired clothes she was wearing when I first met her. The answer to what can I do for her, I guess, is everything. "Sorry," I say and I walk off, not to slab nine though—instead I head back to the office.

"Mom," I say, rapping on the door before opening it. She's sitting on the couch and wiping her eyes. "What's wrong, Ma?"

She gives her head a little shake. "Nuthin'."

"Not nothing, you're crying half the time I see you."

Her face darkens. "Maybe you shouldn't be taking my park away then."

My fingers tighten on the edge of the door, and I'm about to slam it. *Someone's mom recently died.*

"Is it Grandma?"

Her eyes flit toward Grandma's brain. "Hard to be sad when I keep expecting her back, ya know?" Her chest hitches.

"But she's not coming back, is she?" I ask.

"Not in my lifetime. Maybe yours, if she gets what she wants." Tears slip down, and she dries them with a napkin. "What you want, anyways?"

It takes me a second to remember what I came for. "Do you have any clothes, you or Crystal, that you'd mind giving me?"

"You?" she demands.

"Not for me, someone I know." I jerk my head back at camp.

"You talking about that woman with the girl?"

I nod.

She sniffs again and then breaks into a grim smile. "Just leave this one to me."

I hesitate, about to tell her no, leave it to me. And I see the tears are gone. And I recall my goal for the day, to enlist. I nod and start to back down the steps and then stop.

"And, Ma?"

She's already on her feet, headed into Crystal's room. She swallows, waiting.

"Thanks," I say.

As I walk out of there, there's a smile on my face. I didn't do a damn thing, but I'm still smiling. Dalen was right. I've enlisted my first camper. And more campers remain. But the high I get is brief. It's brief because nothing, nothing in all of this has told me the meaning of life. I can't connect the dots. The pool-berg may be a sculpture, but my gut-berg remains a crusty chunk of angst.

Chapter 31

The next morning I wake, but I don't answer Dalen's knock at the door. I bury my face in the pillow. A few minutes later he's managed to jiggle the door enough to open it. He looms over me. I feel leaden, as though I sink into the lumpy mattress.

"What's going on here?" he asks.

I sigh and roll over.

"Better-Ray?"

I shake my head. "Just Ray."

"Explain yourself."

I sigh again. "Well . . . I can see how your spiel is making things happier, better around here, but I still don't see how it's helping me figure out what I should do with my life."

"It's a journey—"

"Screw the journey, I can't start because I have no idea where to go. I want to know *where* I'm going. Should I be a lawyer? A doctor? An artist? What!" I'm sitting up now, heaving. "I have to decide what I want to do, but I suck at almost everything. What can I do?"

Dalen stares at me for a full minute before I look away.

"Tell me about yourself," he asks in a quiet voice. "What are you good at?"

"I'm okay at school, when I want to be, but it's boring so I don't try very hard. I don't know any other languages or nothing. Never really got into sports."

"You're listing excuses and weaknesses," he says. "What are you *good* at?"

I think, but I can't name a thing. Nothing. I'm a pretty good gamer, but I haven't been doing that much. I like flipping burgers, but that's not a career. "Nothing. I'm not even sure I should go back to school. Don't need school to game."

But even gaming I'm not so sure about anymore. Last night I discovered I'd lost another six followers. I'm down to fourteen. Maybe my fans are more important to me than I am to them. Dalen starts to speak, and I know what he's going to say. Stay in school. Education is the key, yadda yadda, so I'm rolling my eyes as he begins.

"Each of us can spend our lifetimes working on our weaknesses. School forces us to do this. You get an F. Do it again. You get an A. Good job, now you don't have to work as hard in that subject, you can focus on what you suck at." As he's talking, his fingers slowly fold into fists. "Did I ever tell you about my daughter?"

I shake my head.

"My daughter's on the autism spectrum. Really struggled. Every day was a grind for her, trying to learn what she had the greatest difficulty with. By the end of the year we would know exactly what her weaknesses were and so would she. It's backwards. Forget about your Fs. So you suck at something.

Admit it, and move on. Learn what you have to, sure, but don't focus on it."

Right now Dalen is saying stuff I'm not sure I'm supposed to hear. Like these are adult secrets. School is broken? It's like he's admitting guilt. And I want him to keep talking.

"Do you know why?" he asks.

"No, why?"

"You can't be anything you want to be, no matter how hard you try."

I'm about to nod again, but stop. "Wait—what? Isn't it supposed to be, I can be whatever I want, I just have to try?"

"No, I'm not going to waste my time or yours. You can't be anything. You going to make the NBA? Be a concert pianist? How about an astronaut? All you need is focus, right?"

"Right, the American Dream."

"Is bullshit."

It's the first time I've heard him swear, and it surprises me.

"The American Dream worked when the government was handing out land, and the dream was to have a good life with a family. It worked when your only other option was to be a priest or a soldier. That's not now. Now you have to find your niche, you have to dig deeper into that niche and be the best of what you can be. Not the best at anything. Not the best at everything."

I fold my arms over my chest.

"Not buying it?" His smile's almost mean. "All you need is perseverance, you're thinking? How good a pianist do you think you could become if you did it day in and day out?" I shrug, but he tells me, "Mediocre. What about a doctoral degree in astrophysics: have you grown up solving puzzles for fun? Maybe you'd get your degree—you're smarter than you know—but that doesn't matter, you'd still be mediocre in the field. You wouldn't be great. What subject do you hate in school?"

"Math," I say.

"You have to work twice as hard at math to get worse grades than the best kid at math in your class, am I right?"

"Ten times as hard," I admit.

"Good, now imagine putting all that effort into something you loved and had some natural talent for. How much better would you be in that subject, or that task? Being great takes work and perseverance, but there are things at which you can never be great. Our culture forces us to invest in so much stuff we suck at. You can be great at who you *are*."

"I can't just do one subject because I only want to do one."

"How old are you?" He knows, so I don't respond. "Who the hell stole from you the magical fairy dust of possibility?" Then he waves his arms. "Ignore that. What would you do at school if you could? One subject." I shake my head again and he frowns. "Where are you holding back?" Dalen demands. "What do you want but tell yourself you can never aspire to have?"

I have an answer, but it's not what he's getting at. It's Tina. I want to confess my feelings to her. But I'm frightened.

I flush.

"Good enough for me," he says. "You've got something going on up there. Now commit to making it happen. Proceed with no caution, like you will die tomorrow, like mistakes are to be expected. Now let's go clean some toilets!"

It's enough to get me out of bed.

Proceedwithnocaution. It's my new password. My mantra.

Chapter 32

For the next hour Dalen and I run through our exercises, but this time when Dalen asks me to visualize, I'm not looking at a picture of my goofy happycamper self, I see me holding Tina, and not in a hey-you're-such-a-good-friend hug. She's embracing me back in an omg-hold-me-close-Better-Ray grip.

Washroom-cleaning meditation, on the other hand, doesn't start well. I have trouble clearing my mind. Shookas turn to shook-shooks as I worry over professing my love to Tina. What if she laughs?

Proceed with no caution.

My mind whirls. I draw steady breaths in the hope that Dalen will think I'm serene and calm. It'll take a miracle for me to go from dork to boyfriend in Tina's eyes. How can I convince her that I'm worthy? Mud and Fire is all about horsepower and testosterone; I need to do something that puts me out there, makes me vulnerable. Something that reflects her interests . . . and I know what it is. Maybe the meditation did work, because I jerk out of the trance knowing what I have to do.

"Who can do it?" Dalen intones.

"I can!" I fist-bump him on my way out of the first washroom and into the next.

Of course, it's barely dawn and I have more cleaning. There's nothing like scrubbing floors and urine from toilet seats to peel unfettered joy from your skull. The overhead fluorescent lights buzz. Flies knock their faces against the mirror. As I scour, I start to hum. It's not one of Tina's made-up melodies. A pop song. Even to my ears it sounds tinny, but I keep scrubbing in rhythm. The morning disappears with the notes of music. By the time I'm done the second washroom, it's my best meditation session ever. I am centered. At peace. And Dalen wasn't even around to witness it.

"The mud's coming along nicely," Obelix says as I step out. "We'll have a good swamp of it for the races."

"Glorious mud," I say.

Campers have dropped logs across the stretch of muck that act like stepping stones across a river.

Mud, mud, glorious mud, I hum and step carefully along the roadside.

I lug the pails of dirty water into the forest to dump them and stop when I hear a squeal. Penny and her mom's trailer stands a little farther down the road, so I stalk through the forest until I'm within sight. Between the trunks of birches, I watch as Penny opens a large cardboard box. The cardboard has been darkened by rainfall. I already can guess what's in it and who left it. Penny's mother holds back, glancing down the road as if hoping to identify the Samaritan.

Penny lifts out Crystal's old teddy bear, a big brown one, thin in spots but it might as well be brand new the way Penny squeezes it. Tears sting my eyes. Then Penny's mom's picks over the contents, holds up soaps and lotions and smiles and digs some more. A jumbo box of tampons excites her way more than I'd ever have expected. I'm really glad I told my mom, and I'm proud of her for doing such an amazing job.

I've never been proud of her in my life.

I slink out of sight and return to scraping the snotties hanging from the shower ceiling. Now I'm singing all out, only quieting when a jack stumbles in with bleary eyes, but I don't stop. I clean the showers better than they've ever been cleaned; even the calcified showerheads glisten. I draw a deep breath of moist, citrus-scented air and strike up what I can recall of some Adele songs.

I began my rounds of the camp yesterday evening so hit the rest of it this morning when a different shift is returning or waking. My own enlightenment has not transferred to the camp, and most of what I receive from campers are complaints about the mud, the bugs, the lack of food options. I have another noise complaint, this one from a woman who sleeps between two night-shift workers. I ask her if she'd be willing to switch slabs with Buck. The move happens within minutes of my suggestion. Buck, red-eyed from his shift, claps me on the shoulders and asks if he can give me a tip.

I finish my office chores and go to vacuum the pool's sides, still giddy with the success of the day.

The ice bear has melted some, the rough hacks smoothed by the warmth. Facets shed rainbows across the gray concrete. I brush down the sides of the pool and the bottom. It clouds with algae and I go back to the shed and pick up the chlorine, dumping a healthy dose into the pool before I start the pump to filter and circulate the water. Penny's there watching the chlorine fumes pour off the surface.

"Did you just make it hot?" she asks in awe.

"No, it's stuff to clean it."

"So I can swim?"

"Not yet."

"You said tomorrow."

"I know. I know." I snap a little and then calm down, shaking it off. "The air's warm now. I figure it'll be another day and then you can swim in it."

"One more sleeps."

"Yeah, one more sleep."

She starts to walk away and then stops, turns, "You always say that and then after the sleep you say it again," she says. "Why do you lie?"

"It wasn't—I'm not a—I didn't mean it as a lie," I say. "We get busy, and other things are sometimes more important."

"More important than the lying," she says and, as she walks away, she adds, "I hate it here."

It's like the good parts of this morning never even happened. I swallow the guilt and empty the pool filter, including two dead moles. Shiny black coats glisten, lifeless corpses but with near-magical snouts, fingers on the tip acting as their way of exploring the world. I'm doing what I can. *Proceed.* I hear Dalen's order— my mantra. *I can.*

I bury the moles in the playground sand, and then creep up on Pulled Beef and peer over the counter.

On the floor of the trailer, Tina sits with one of Dalen's books in her lap. She's taking notes. My heart starts to pound. A warm flush prickles over me as I crouch beneath the counter.

Then I hear her banging around in the fridge.

This is my chance. It even fits the lyrics of the song. I begin to sing "Hello" by Adele. The moment I start, silence fills Pulled Beef. Even a nearby jack scraping a barbecue grill stops to listen. It's a love song. It's a beautiful song, but of course I'm tearing it to pieces with my voice. I strain for every high note, and crackle over the lows. I must have listened to the karaoke version a half-billion times, but my version's a little like listening to the cows waiting at a slaughterhouse.

But I'm trying. And caution's in the wind, bending the tops of pine trees.

From the road Crystal shakes her head. I give her a little wave and then her eyes widen. She grins and points. It's not at me. Above my head. I sense Tina leaning out over the counter. I smile, which actually helps me hit an especially high note, but it's not her. It's Salminder. I falter.

Crystal cackles and walks on.

"Why, thank you, Ray," Salminder says.

"Supreme dork!" Tina yells from inside. The trailer door swings open. She sprints through it, not looking back. I start to clamber up after her, but Salminder's hand's on my head, shoving me back down.

"Let her go," he says. But still I struggle, the day toppling down around me. As I fight to my feet, I wrench away, my elbow catching Salminder on the side of his head. A fat purple turban falls to the mud at my feet. I stop.

"Damn," Salminder says. And he lunges for it. "Will you get

that for me, please," he whispers and then retreats into the shadows of the truck.

"I'm so sorry," I say, holding the turban up and then rushing inside to give it to him when he doesn't come forward.

"Without hair, the turban doesn't stay on quite as well," he explains. "It's the treatments."

His hair's scraggly and patchy, his beard and eyebrows too. Without all that hair, he seems smaller, fragile even. "Your hair, I'm sorry, that's important, right? You're not supposed to cut it."

"Not since the day I was born." He's rewrapping the turban on his head, trying to tighten the cloth and wipe away the smear of mud. "My hair, my Kesh, forms part of my connection to God. It is a manifestation of my love for Him, and my link to Guru Nanak. Its loss is not an affront, but a sadness."

"I'm sorry, I didn't know you were here."

"It's okay, but maybe . . ." His smile is sad. "Perhaps now is not the time to confuse Tina with this." I nod, my throat tight. "Please, excuse me."

He keeps one hand on his headgear as he follows in the tracks of his daughter. This is big; for years, Salminder's been like a father to me, but his loyalty lies with his daughter. I've forced our relationship to change.

I slump to the ground, tears in my eyes. I'm angry at myself for being so selfish. At Dalen for convincing me to do this. *Don't assign blame—yeah, right.* Dalen's book is open, and written on the bookmark are Tina's notes.

Steps to Meaning:
Set goals
Control your negative thoughts

Meditate

Visualize your success

Keep your promises

Live your days as if they are your last

Remember the golden rule

Beside each item in the list is a column of famous people. Some ancient like Jesus, Buddha, Muhammad, Lao Tzu, others a bit more modern, Martin Luther King, and then Tony Robbins, Robin Sharma, Oprah Winfrey.

Thoughts lead to actions, actions to habit, habit to destiny. <===*Gandhi? Buddha?*

I see what she's done. She's noted who Dalen's stealing his sayings from. Dalen's nothing more than a plagiarist. A fraud. It's all spiritual guru karaoke.

I don't like it.

Chapter 33

I'm listening to some nine-year-old sing "Hello" when Dalen taps me on the shoulder.

"You all right?" he asks.

I want to call him out, but I bite my tongue—I need to catch Dalen at the right time, when he's repeated something irrefutably not his.

I pull the headphones down to hang them around my neck. My stomach roils from the old box of Kraft Dinner I'd discovered under the sink. It was not an afternoon of champions. I'd eaten a couple of burgers while waiting for Tina to return. She never did. Salminder took her shift, said he wanted to since he had another chemo session tomorrow and wouldn't be around to help out. But I know the real reason. I'd embarrassed Tina. It confirmed my dorkage.

I stare back at the computer screen and the kid singing his face off.

"This guy's like three years old and he sings better than I ever will. Elephants paint better than I can. And I'm going to take a wild guess that I can find people out there better at everything than me. Why focus on anything when there's no way I have a chance at being the best at it?"

Dalen scratches his head for a moment, and I think of Salminder and how weird it must feel for him not to have any hair. How powerless he must feel.

"You're right."

"Great. More tough love," I say.

"There is one other secret I'll let you in on," Dalen says, in his I'm-going-to-tell-you-something-important voice. "Comparison is poison."

I shrug and bite back, "Like comparing yourself to Jesus or Buddha?"

He frowns at me.

"Not really what I meant . . ." When I don't explain, he continues. "Well, a couple hundred years ago, who would you have known? How would you have gotten your news if you lived back then?"

I frown. "I'd probably have been on a farm, so my family, and maybe we'd get news from the next couple of farms over. I dunno? Trips to town for gossip."

"Local gossip. Maybe a small-town newspaper. And it would be infrequent. Good. And what about when your mom was a kid?"

"County fair? Newspaper, no—radio and television, right?" I'm thinking about those pixelated newscasts.

"Did she know that some kid in Japan had figured out how to create a robotic arm? Or that a five-year-old played Bach in the UK?"

"Probably not." The kid in the video's fingers are dancing

over the strings of the guitar, and I can hear the thin warbling of his song through the headphones on the table.

"No. She came in third at the cross-country race. She fell in love with the second best-looking boy in school. She was good at math. Get it?" I shake my head. "Her frame of reference was smaller. She was the big fish in a small pond. Today, with the Internet, the small pond is now an ocean. If your mom was a kid now, she'd have seen that her third place in her tiny school wouldn't have put her in the top thirty percent of runners, or her math skills wouldn't get her into even the worst Ivy League schools, or put her on track to being a Google engineer. Her boyfriend wasn't all that good-looking, not when compared to the models you see everywhere now. Comparison is poison. The poison is available at any time. It detracts from very real accomplishments and it hides all the steps and hardships required along the way to any achievement, even the hard work required from a prodigy. The trick is to look inward. Did you do your best, did you beat your own best time? Do you understand your math? Be your own pond."

"Be your own pond." I actually type it into Google Search to see who he stole the concept from as he gabs on. I get nothing.

"Conquer yourself. Exactly."

"But isn't it all just a matter of what you tell yourself?"

"Yes!" He pumps his fist.

"But aren't we lying to ourselves then?" On the screen I can see that many people have riffed on the "Conquer yourself" concept, Buddha and Plato among them.

Dalen starts to say something, then stops. He holds up his hand, shakes it at me, and then breathes heavily from his nose.

"Okay," he says, "try this. Imagine there's a nationwide competition. And you get an A in your high school. You go on to compete for the whole region of say ten high schools, and again, you get an A in that group too. Then it's ten regions competing and you get another A. Half the country, and still you get an A. It's down to you and a hundred other kids in a final class. If you get an A, you will be one of the best students in the whole country. You work so hard and finally you come out with a D. You're devastated, right?"

"Yeah."

"Yes, and some of the kids got Fs too. They failed."

"Sucks to be them."

"That's what the problem is. That kid who got the F. He is the ninety-ninth best student in the entire country, and he feels like a failure because he came in second to last. He may never become that amazing engineer or physicist because while he's comparing himself to the ten smartest kids, he's forgetting what makes him different. When the news and the Internet only endlessly cover the exceptions, the one in a million, it makes everyone else feel like failures."

"Yeah, but, that's the way it works. You make money, you're successful. Get a degree, I dunno, maybe become a senator. That's how you know you're doing it right," I say.

"Stop measuring. Life is *your* video game. You're talking about the measurements of society—that's a crappy game. Choose your own labels and stories. They are all made up anyways. Remember that tulip you saw? If you lived in seventeenth-century Denmark, that tulip might have been worth tens of thousands of dollars. Measurements are like grades, degrees, money in the bank: all of it is for people who do not control their destinies. They are controlled by those around them. I'm not saying don't be hard on yourself. Learn languages. Instruments, or the fine art of finance. These are wondrous achievements, but mastery is not an A. It's so much greater than that. Embrace your progression to mastery. Move forward and do not look to the external for approval. Let your inner joy carry you."

"Mastery over measurement," I say, coming up with my new password for the day.

Sadness seems to make Dalen's head heavy as it waggles on his neck. He inspects the lines on his palms.

"Not learning that message destroyed my marriage. It lost me my daughter. I always wanted more. To achieve more. It was never enough and never would be. Until my wife left me, and I realized that the game I played was all wrong. It wasn't even a game I wanted to play.

"Growing up today and being compared to YouTube stars and child millionaires, I wouldn't know where to start. Most of us are not exceptions, but all of us can become exceptional. We become exceptional by not playing by the Internet's rules and labels."

"Make my own emojis? You know, the smiley faces."

His head snaps up and I face that fierceness in his eyes. I hold it.

"Exactly," he says.

And I do see, because I've done it. I've looked at lots of kids with millions of views on YouTube playing their guitars. Or heard about kids starting companies and making millions by the time they were seventeen. I've wondered what's wrong with me, rather than what's right with me.

I want to confront him for stealing the wisdom of all the people on Tina's bookmark, but the bitterness has ebbed. The video's over, and YouTube's picked another prodigy for me to feel inadequate in comparison. Still, there's something wrong with what he's saying, but it's elusive.

"Charlie's invited you to dinner," Dalen says. "That's why I'm here."

I point to the pot of congealing KD. I'm not sure how far to trust Dalen anymore. I wonder whether I'm being brainwashed and need some space. The whole proceeding without caution thing didn't work out so well with Tina. "Sorry," I say. "I'm full up, and besides, Obelix and I are working on Mud tonight."

Dalen eyes me for a minute. "Rain check," he says.

"Dalen?" I ask. I have it. I see his hypocrisy. "You said not to measure, but didn't you say I wasn't worth helping because others could make a bigger difference?"

Dalen looks down and takes a deep breath. "Even gurus can be wrong," he says and heads out into the drizzle.

There's another knock on the door. I figure it's Obelix, and I don't care if he sees me in my underwear, so I shout for him to come on in.

Penny just laughs as I struggle to find a towel to cover up.

"Hey, hey," I say as I pull the blanket off the tiny love seat in the back. The blanket had been hiding a gash, and sponge pops from between the lips of the tear.

"Pool's ready!" she says. "My mom says I can go in if you go with me."

I hesitate, but there's this look in her eyes that says she's living in the moment, and this is maybe the moment when she learns that adults won't always let her down.

I shuffle over to the closet where I keep my clothes and pull on swim trunks beneath the towel. Then I say, "Race you there." And she squeals again.

Chapter 34

"Not today," I say and push Dalen aside as I open the door to my trailer before he has a chance to rat-a-tat-tat on it.

"Good luck, Ray," he says to my back. "I'd be willing to say a few words at the event if you'd like."

I hustle down the path as he trails off. I've been up all night working with Obelix on Mud and Fire. Sunny Days' first ever race. To encourage participation, we set it between two mine shifts in the early evening.

The gun fires at 5:00 p.m. I have to do everything else beforehand. I sprint to the cleaning products, taking a long route to avoid Tina's trailer, telling myself that I'm inspecting the race course. Salminder's back in the hospital, but I can't bring myself to face Tina. I'm pretty sure she doesn't want to talk to me anyway.

Sloshing some detergent into a pail with water, I start on the women's washroom before anyone arrives. There are eight stalls and six sinks, and each takes a few minutes to clean. I start with the sinks. I've decided that doing them after the toilets is kind of gross. An hour later, the floor shines. I shrug as a woman tromps in, clods of mud peeling from her boots. Nothing lasts forever. And you can't have Mud and Fire without actual mud.

I can't decide whether I'm more excited about the Mud or the Fire part.

"Get out of here, kid," the woman says with a hand on the stall door.

"Oh, sorry, just thinking."

"Could've fooled me—don't let me catch you peeking."

The woman's big, has a foot on me in every direction; could've taken Grandma's bear. I wonder what Grandma would have thought of the Mud and Fire event. Is this what she meant by doing something with my life? Her recipe? The woman grunts, and I waddle out with the pails to dump them in the woods. Then I repeat the process with the men's washrooms and showers. My mother, who seems to have nothing better to do, watches from her lawn furniture. The expression on her face tells me that the glow of having helped Penny and her mother has long ago faded.

The sun isn't quite out, but the rain stopped last night.

Sixteen pickup trucks are signed up to compete, and a very surprising twelve ATVs. Over half the signups are care of Deneze, who rallied the rez to participate. The trucks will be timed around the course, which weaves through the park along all the roadways. Fastest time wins. The ATVs will run in two separate heats. Top three from each will move to the final. I'm the starter and Obelix is the race official, except when he's racing his truck, which I catch him polishing.

Dalen heads me off when I'm dumping my pails.

"Tonight, Ray." The guy looks, of all things, nervous. "Can

I go out there? Can I have a chance to speak to the audience?"

He's twitching and scratching at his arms.

"Is it like an addiction for you?" I ask. "Public speaking?"

"No, no, not at all, public speaking terrifies me, actually. But you were right. About how I'd started using the wrong measurements. This is as a chance for me to change that. My time here's been an eye-opener for me. I've been more energized. Helping a real case. *You.* You'd be floundering without me, right?"

"Thanks, yeah, but I still don't know the meaning of life."

"I only mean, I can see the difference I'm making, and now I want to help everyone."

I frown.

"I promise to keep it short. I am also willing to make it entirely complimentary."

He bops up and down. A sheen of desperation shines in his eyes.

"I guess."

"Great! How about 'Mud, Fire, and Firing You Up with Dalen Anders'?"

"Maybe next time," I say.

"Right, right, no time to change the media you've sent out."

"Media, yeah, I wish." I roll my eyes.

He claps his hands together and says, "Don't worry, Ray, I can help there."

He is off to his bus before I have a chance to ask what he means. I start to follow him, but a teary Tina shuts the door on the office. She's been using the phone. I freeze, and so does she, except for the tears. Those keep coming.

I walk up to her. *Supreme dork.* Realizing that it's not all about me, I ask, "How's your dad doing?" She collapses into my arms. "What? What?"

She steps back, looks to the sky and then blows out her cheeks with each heaving breath.

"He had an . . . they call it an adverse reaction," she cries and clutches me around the neck.

"Is he okay?" I hold her close.

"I spoke to him—he doesn't want me to see him like this. Says he's fine but won't be home today."

"Okay, then, all right." I'm thinking fast for some way to console her. It can't be good if the drugs that are supposed to kill your disease are killing you instead. If he's okay, though, what she really needs is a distraction. "Say, uh, wanna help with Mud and Fire? I could sure use it."

She nods a snuffly nose into my shirt. It leaves a snail trail, but I'm not really one to worry about dirty clothes. When my question's out it sounds more selfish, but I babble on as we head over to Pulled Beef. I'm hyperaware of my hand on her shoulder blade.

"Mud is bigger than I ever hoped it could be. Truck and ATV races. Uncle Jamie's doing this fireworks display at night. We'll need lots and lots of burgers. Let's try to beat the record? Okay?"

"Is Crystal racing her ATV?" she asks.

"No, I haven't seen her. I think she's after the bear."

She nods. "Okay."

I leave her grilling patties and miss the warmth of her skin against my hand.

My mother says nothing as I pass her and climb into the office to do the bare minimum of paperwork before I rush back out a half an hour later.

I shut my eyes. I hear everything. Obelix clearing the course, asking campers to keep furniture and vehicles well on to their lots; some woman sings in the shower. The pop of grease. The bass beat of a dance song thumps as someone does a chore of their own. It's the music of the RV park. The swing set squeals. I smile at Penny, who stares back, waving with fingers that grip the rusting chain.

I can do this. I own this. It may not be the meaning of life, but it's something.

The rumble of a truck arriving overwhelms all else. Mud and Fire—it's here.

Actually.

It's early.

Chapter 35

The first pickup truck arrives at noon, but to call it a "truck" is like calling Big Mountain "a hill." The monster sits atop a raised chassis with tires as tall as I am. They rub against the gate posts as they ease into the park. Stenciled on its bright yellow hood is the name *Golden Nugget*. A woman hops out, swings down to hang from the running board and then lands in the mud.

"Saw the news release," she says. "Where's the track?" I'm just staring, wide-eyed. "Hello? Where's the course? Who's running this thing?" she asks.

"Sorry, looking at him," I say, glancing at a tire and trying to determine if the truck is going to fit down the road. "The park's the track."

Her smile broadens. "Demolition? I get to run over those?"

"What? The trailers? No, no," I say, imagining how easily Golden Nugget's wheels could crush the RVs. "It's the road."

Maybe she sees how anxious I am because she says, "Don't worry, I'll go easy on the racers. But I better make sure I can handle those turns."

I nod and she lowers a ladder to climb back in.

Blue smoke pumps from the chrome exhaust pipes that hug the cab. The truck idles down the first road, a foot to spare on either side. Obelix jiggles up and down, hooting.

"Can you believe who it is? Can you?"

I can't. "Did you send out a press release?" I ask, but Obelix is running to the next road over to catch another glimpse of the monster truck.

The second truck arrives ten minutes later. Stars riddle the glossy black paint. Neither of these trucks is on my list of entries. Something's happened. I jog to where Dalen's bus is tucked just outside of camp. A broad satellite dish perches on top. Charlie lets me up.

"Hi, Charlie." She smiles at me before going back to reading her Kindle. I hear Dalen practicing his speech.

"Who can do it?" he asks. "I can't hear you . . . who can do it?" He gives himself a round of applause. "You can! Crowd roars. Dalen, Dalen, Dal—!"

He catches sight of me.

"Only a couple minutes, right?" I say. "That's all you'll have."

"I can read audiences, Ray, don't worry." He holds out calming hands. "I won't hog the mic."

I frown.

"Did you issue a press release about Mud and Fire?"

He nods frantically and gives a thumbs-up. "You're welcome! Did you know that people pay upward of a thousand dollars to attend my workshops? Hey, I'm happy to help. But don't worry. I am sure some of the people who come will be here for the truck race."

Panic-berg must have been hiding in my gut, because it does

a flip to remind me of its presence. I quake with anger, but Dalen's back to rehearsing. There's nothing to be done about the press release now. It explains the new arrivals. Another pair of souped-up trucks roar down the road, downshifting, engines growling. These are pros—*Monster Muck* and *Deadly Delilah* are written on their respective hoods.

There goes my afternoon.

I start registering new competitors, sorting out timing and figuring out where to park everyone. By three o'clock, the road into camp's blocked. Almost fifty competitors are already registered, and more are waiting—and that's only the trucks. Spectators hoof it in, lugging camping chairs and coolers. Obelix is nearly peeing his pants, hopping up and down as he lines people up along the course. A news helicopter swivels overhead.

"Gear up, Tina," I say, as I pass by Pulled Beef. "As many burgers as you can, just make them up, you'll sell out in an hour." She nods, a focused look on her face. At the very least, she's keeping so busy she barely has time to think about her father. As I walk away I realize she's humming. It's the song I'd tried to sing. The melody lifts on the morning's light wind and me along with it, as if I'd never attempted to profess my love to her. The bear sculpture shines in the sun. The chainsaw and chisel marks have smoothed in the heat.

When I rush by my mother, she folds her arms across her chest.

"Should be charging," she says. "And you gots two toilets plugged."

"You want to file a tenant's complaint?" I demand. It's hard to believe the clouds could drift over my soul so quickly, but here

I stand and glower. The sculpture's still at my back, the song still on the air, but there's a dark scowl on my face.

Her back straightens as her lips push out but, soon after, her shoulders roll. Head hangs. There's more that I want to say. This whole thing hasn't been my fault. It isn't just *her* summer Grandma's dying ruined. *Is* ruining. And somehow I sense that if I strike at her now, it'll be over. She'll fold her tent. I'll have won.

"Mama," I say. She's shaking her head, but keeping it all bent like it's ready for my guillotine.

Once, when I was little, a turtle with a cracked shell writhed on the road. It had been run over but still lived. Grandma had been driving her pickup and, when I pointed it out, she hammered the brakes so fast I slammed into the dashboard. She leaped from the truck, waving at the oncoming traffic to slow, yelling for me to save the turtle. I ran over to it and stood above it. Its neck strained like my mom's now, the turtle's expression the same grimace my mother wears. I pulled the turtle to the side of the road and shoved it into the ditch. Never knew what happened to the little guy.

"Would you help me?" I ask my mother. "I could really use some help."

Her neck lifts.

"No toilets," she says, but the edge in her tone has blunted. I know that if I ask her to clean the toilets, she will.

"You're in charge of crowd and ATV control," I say instead. The ATVs buzz in the background, ripping up the sides of the roads and slithering through the mud between trucks.

Her arms are folded across her chest again. "Well, since you asked. And since I want a camp left when I take it back, I'll help."

If she'd kept talking, I might have told her to forget it, but she didn't. She always seems to know how far she can push me.

By 4:30, my mom has assigned the audience the same numbers as those on trailer slabs. They're setting up their chairs. I haven't seen a fist fight in at least five minutes. Obelix has ranked all the competitors that can squeeze through the traffic jam. Deneze straddles his ATV near all the friends he registered. They've been pushed off to the side as if they're some street gang. They lounge on their hefty four-wheelers.

"You okay, Ray?" Deneze asks.

I nod. "Yeah, stay cool," I say.

"We're cool if they're cool."

"They" are another group of riders, from town. The simmering competition between rez jobs and contracts, and townie jobs and contracts, holds no bounds, and winning today will be about far more than a trophy for them.

Trophy. I don't even have a trophy. What are these people here for? There's no prize money, nothing to put on a mantel. At least no "pro" ATVers have arrived.

"Get something started," Deneze recommends. "Before someone else does."

I grab the megaphone my mom's been using to shout her demands. "Mom, figure out how to keep the townies from brawling with Deneze's crew . . . please," I say quietly, just to her, and she struts off. After a deep breath, I announce, "Dalen Anders, Dalen Anders will be speaking at the starting line, come listen to our very own celebrity."

The clapping's more muted than I expected, but Dalen exits

the bus like a billion dollars, all teeth and shooting his shirt cuffs. He picks his way carefully through all the mud, leaping to dry spots like a deer.

"Who can do it?" he hollers, the question ridden over by the roar of an engine.

The stage is the back of Obelix's pickup. Dalen hops on up and lifts his arms to the crowd. I hand him the megaphone.

Whether to see Dalen or because they have nothing better to do, people drift toward the silver GMC pickup, many clutching burgers in their hands. Tina must be crushed beneath the weight of orders.

"Thank you, thank you for coming!" Dalen yells. "Welcome to Mud, Fire, and Firing It Up with Dalen Anders!"

Over the sporadic applause he starts his patter.

"Who here feels aimless?" He doesn't really wait for an answer, just nods at the audience as if they're all nodding back too. They're not. "Feel guilty about not achieving more? Uh-huh, guilt is the emotion of the past.

"Who here's fought with their spouse? Say aye." He smiles at the muttered "ayes." "How about your girlfriend or boyfriend? Of course you have. You're tired. You're frustrated. Sometimes you think—this isn't the life I wanted. I want more! But I'm stuck!"

This doesn't feel like a two-minute beginning. Obelix has the trucks lined up, one after the other. It's remarkable really, given there's so little room to maneuver. Only half of the audience is following Dalen; the others snap pictures of the first truck at the start line. A portly man, decked out in full leathers that sparkle, signs autographs. His machine looks more tire than truck and sports a big multi-eyed blower on the hood.

"I'm here to tell you the secrets of ancients," Dalen says, his voice loud to compete with the trucks. "The wisdom that has come to me after years of meditation."

This garners more interest. People stop talking to one another and stare up at Dalen. Who doesn't want to know secrets? I understand. I did, too.

"Who here drinks too much? Watches too much TV? Smokes, but wants to stop?" The smokers in the camp seem to draw in a single sharp breath of exhaust-filled air. "How about those extra pounds? Who doesn't have a few of those they'd rather not be carrying around?"

There's an angry buzz and laughter in the wrong places. What's gone wrong?

"These are symptoms, folks, symptoms and analgesics of an unfulfilled life!"

He has their attention, but I'm not sure it's the sort anyone wants, all tight eyes and lips. These people, I realize, they're not here for "Firing It Up with Dalen Anders," they're here for "Mud and Fire." When Dalen arrived at Sunny Days, it was because *I* called him. I was open to his messages; this crowd's just anxious for the starter gun.

"I've traveled the jungles of Borneo. The mountains of Northern India. I've studied with ancient orders of monks, and today I bring you insights and secrets. Are you ready?"

He stumbles, and the megaphone emits a piercing shriek. By my watch he's already had his two minutes. Even I can read this crowd. In my head, I'm thinking—*Give these guys a secret, a good one, now!*

"Why do you race? The thrill. To feel. Am I right? When you're racing, you're in the moment. And that's where you should always be. Every day you should wake excited, with a little vomit in your mouths." Dalen laughs. "And yet, you what? You run off to your shifts at the mines, don't you? Day in day out, the same job. You feel guilty about the past and yearn for the future. You're never in the present."

One of the jacks steps close to the stage and says, "I like my job."

"Me, too," comes another.

"I don't," one man says, "but if I didn't do it my family would starve."

Dalen hones in on this man as if seeing a problem he can solve. "Your only limitations, my friend, are those you place on yourself." He smiles around at snarling eyes. "Yes, you can. Who can do it?"

There's silence, and then, "My limitations are an empty bank account and hungry kids," a woman says.

"Our thoughts are our own prisons. If you can see it, you can be it!" Dalen yells.

"Start the race!" someone shouts. I'm running for the tailgate where Dalen stands, his arms out, confused.

"Start the race!" Others take up the call.

"See this!" Booing starts, and a clod of mud catches Dalen on the shoulder. He falls back like he's been punched. I can see the hurt in his eyes, even though he keeps smiling as he rolls to the gate and down out of the truck. I don't have time to console him. He doesn't seem to need it, anyway.

"Tough crowd," he mutters to me. "Megaphone isn't working properly."

But I'm with the crowd. What's more, I'm the one who asked this guy to come. I let him speak. I'm responsible, and right now I'm wondering if Dalen knows any secrets at all. Like really? See it, be it? Actions lead to habits and habits to destiny? Throw in some meditation. Really? Here's his message: If life sucks, it's because I think sucky thoughts. Sucky thoughts lead to doing suckage. Too much suckage and I will have a sucky destiny. So don't suck.

"Is anything you say yours?" I ask. "Really yours? Or are you like a regurgitating guru?"

More chunks of mud sail over the truck and strike the trailer behind. Dalen blanches, but I don't have time for him.

I jump up, dodge dirt, and then shout into the megaphone, "Are you ready for the main event?"

The door of the first truck slams. Obelix hands me the starter gun. I grab the heavy steel.

A cheer roars. This isn't a tough crowd, not at all. They came for Mud and Fire. They came to forget about life and have fun for a couple of hours. Same as I do with my gaming. How about this? How about, too much thinking about the meaning of life leads to not enough fun. Not enough fun leads to an angry mob.

"Get to your seats!" my mom shouts, and the people disperse.

The truck revs its engine as Dalen glances back one final time. But I have nothing for him. He's the one who turned my race into a monster truck event. I'd only wanted to make the campers happy and fix the roads.

Dalen doesn't pick his way through the mud, from dry patch to dry patch; he slops into the deepest areas, mud wallowing around his knees. His feet are bare, shoes lodged somewhere in the muck.

I lift the gun. The truck spins its rear tires, showering the truck behind it in sludge.

I pull the trigger.

Chapter 36

BANG!

When the recoil flips the gun barrel back into my cheek, I realize it's not a starter gun. It's real. The helicopter that had been hovering nearby veers away to a safe distance. Luckily, no one else was in the sky.

The truck rips down the lane, and mud waves over the crowd, which falls back. Those farther along the road retreat as the truck approaches. It skids on the turn, hits a tree that shudders and then passes out of sight. Cheers lift on the other side of camp.

"You timing?" Obelix's big lips are stretched wide and up like a crazy Cheshire Cat. I swear and start my watch. "It's all right, I got it."

The next truck rattles as it nears. This one's battered and rusted where not coated in slick mud. I wipe blood from where the gun barrel nicked me. Then I glance around to see where the helicopter is, or any passing ducks. And fire the pistol into the air.

I don't know what goes wrong with the truck, but pistons slam into its hood and it rolls, smoking to the side of the course.

Even as I scream in surprise, the crowd cheers. The first competitor makes the fourth and final turn, running hot toward the finish line, which is a bit too close to the start line for comfort.

I motion the next truck forward, the woman first to arrive— Golden Nugget. I lift the gun and shoot, getting the hang of the buck of the kickback. The incoming truck nearly clips Golden Nugget. Obelix stops his watch before recording the time. If I had Dalen to talk to, I'd tell him my new goal for the day: that no one gets hurt.

Over the course of the next couple hours, fifty trucks throw most of the mud to the sides of the course. Nothing escapes the muck. In places, the road's down to the bedrock beneath, but with one exception, a large hump in the middle. Some of the smaller trucks with lower clearance can't manage the hump and require a tow off.

After the last truck races, I go to check on Tina. Well after eight o'clock, Pulled Beef should be packed. Luckily the combination of exhaust and mud are pushing away the bugs. But Tina's gone, having left Penny to sell a few dozen premade burgers. Penny won't tell me where Tina went. I hope Salminder's all right.

Aside from Dalen's bruised ego, it appears as though we might make it through unscathed, but next are the ATVs. The townies and Deneze's crew have stewed in the mud bath, awaiting their turn under my mom's watchful glare. I note that a few on each side are so covered in mud they could only have been wrestling in it.

"They's been wrestling in it," my mom says.

I have to start their race. "ATVs to the starting line," I announce through the megaphone.

My mom split the groups into the two cohorts, and these run without incident. But that still means three of each in a hotly contested final. I watch my mother, a foot shorter than some of the drivers; she's in her element, born to order and to organize. When I took over the camp from her, I didn't just take her inheritance, I realize—I took what made her happy. Once I catch her looking at me, too. Not with the usual open hostility, but rather with pride. That makes me uncomfortable.

Why *are* the racers here? The spectators? My mom was right; they would have spent money to be here. Is it just because it's something to do? Is it to forget the lack of meaning in their lives, or does this all somehow offer meaning? The truck drivers congratulate the winner, the woman in Golden Nugget, now covered in mud. Obelix came in fortieth, but smiles as though he won.

If death is the outcome of life's race, then who really wins? As the six ATV finalists idle to the starting line in their quads, they're evenly divided between rez members and townies.

I nod to Deneze in his distinctive green helmet, but he doesn't nod back. His visor is fixed on the course.

The extra competitors have pushed the races into the late evening. A good crowd should remain for the fireworks. I catch the splash of someone in the pool. And then the engine noise overwhelms all else.

I pull the trigger.

The ATVs leap into the troughs. Deneze rips up the side of the hump and claims the peak, accelerating even as one of the townies slides halfway up and, on a forty-five-degree angle, speeds after him, slipping past the other riders. After that, townies and rez members mix. One spins out. I glance back at my mom's trailer. Crystal's ATV is gone from the side. I peer again at the racers. I have no idea who is who with the other four, but I do know that the ATV chasing Deneze is my sister's. Where'd she come from? I lose sight as they disappear around the bend.

The crowd's cheers follow the leaders. I rush to the edge of the road where they'll race to the finish. Around the second turn, Deneze skids and moves behind Crystal's ATV before surging after it. At the final bend Deneze, back in the lead, takes the turn tight, but whoever's driving Crystal's ATV was trying to cut him off and veers sharply behind him. *Too* sharply.

The ATV fires over the hump and launches, soars over the heads of ducking spectators, and hits the ground grill first. The driver tumbles into the heavy grasses. Deneze tears over to the side and sprints to check on the racer, while the other ATVs, unaware of what has happened, shoot past to the finish line.

I ignore the race and head for the accident. Deneze shakes out his long dark hair and grins down at the figure in the grass. Someone reaches up with a gloved hand, clasps his forearm and stands. Relief washes over me, and then I freeze. The rider leans heavily on Deneze, who speaks before the rider nods back.

The rider pulls off her helmet.

"Tina?" I whisper.

Her hair's wild with sweat, face stunned, red, and deliriously happy. She comes to focus on me, shrugs, and gives me the thumbs-up. Deneze claps her on the back before steadying her again. I want to go to her but the race is over, and I'm the guy with the megaphone standing in the biggest ruts this trailer park has ever seen.

Nothing has escaped the mud, but everyone smiles. Even the townies and rez members clasp hands and laugh.

I put the megaphone to my lips. "The *mud* portion of Mud and Fire is over. *Fire* begins in half an hour." Weary from the day, many people begin to leave, but Obelix blocks them and I remember how this all began. "One last task. Many hands make light work, folks. Grab a shovel and let's smooth these ruts!"

Obelix distributes as many rakes and shovels as he has found. Those without an implement use their boots. Soon hundreds of spectators are kicking and shoveling away at the road, doing their best to repair it. My mom watches with a grin on her face. *Community.* That's what this is about. *The pack.* I search for Tina, but she's gone. Instead I find Uncle Jamie, pale and quaking, holding what looks more like cannons than fireworks.

It's time for fire.

Chapter 37

"What's the matter, Uncle Jamie?" I ask.

He gives his head a fractional shake. "Wish there wasn't quite so many people. Maybe we should start with a smaller group? Wait until more people leave?"

"Don't be afraid of failure, Uncle Jamie. It's not about how many times the fireworks blow up in your face, it's about trying until they don't, right?"

I'd meant it as a joke really, but Uncle Jamie nods, and I realize I just Dalen'ed him. Come to think of it, the little girl—Penny—had said something that had sounded Dalenish to me, too. I correct myself. They aren't Dalenisms. They're cobbled together from other people—if they're secrets, then they were someone else's secrets long before and are secrets anyone can read or hear.

"Each one," Uncle Jamie says, nodding to the firework tubes, "has one shot. I don't know if any of them will work. There's no testing them without using them. Understand?"

And I do. Each one is a little life. One shot each, and there's no testing to see which recipe will result in the best bang. "It'll be awesome," I add, and with the rockets stacked in his arms like firewood, he heads toward the gate and launch zone.

Music draws me to Pulled Beef. Tina sings and flips and makes each burger, spinning once as she offers the burger to the customer with an unfettered smile I haven't seen for a while. Another camper helps at the grill. I think it's the one who does the shadow puppets. Penny makes change. I grin at them. "Fireworks in a few minutes," I tell the people in line. "You won't want to miss it."

My eyeballs itch from lack of sleep. I long for sustenance. I'm stretched. As I leave, Penny tugs at my T-shirt and hands me a burger. "One double Swami," she says. "I see a full tummy in your future."

"Thanks, Penny, why don't you watch the fireworks from here, okay? Just to be safe."

She nods.

Ahead there's a crackle, and lightning zigzags through the air, leaving a cloud of white smoke. The sun's low. Not quite low enough for darkness, but low enough that if the fireworks shoot high enough, they'll be framed in midnight blue.

Uncle Jamie skitters from tube to tube, digging with a small trowel to set the fireworks into the ground, angling them to shoot out over the swamp and not the campground. The crowd keeps pressing him. "Get back!" He waves, but as soon as he turns to the tubes, the audience shifts forward again. "You don't understand, danger . . . danger . . . ," he says.

There's no need to announce the start. Uncle Jamie sees me, clicks a barbecue starter and lights a fuse. He sprints from it, well beyond the crowd, dives and covers his head.

Smoke spits from the tube's mouth. The audience watches, eyes wide. Someone snickers. Another mockingly *ohs* and *ahs* at the odd sparks that spit out. But I watch in horror as I follow the sparks. Sparks that land near three nearby rockets. Their fuses flare one after the other.

"No, no," Jamie cries and scrambles even farther back. The first blast actually manages to lift far enough from the ground that it waggles into the swamp before snuffing out.

The second flies far into the night, where it simply disappears. But the fuse of the final firework sizzles as it burns into the red painted tube and then . . . nothing.

The crowd leans forward in total silence. Even I, who have seen my uncle's shed explode a dozen times, edge into the circle.

"Back!" Jamie shouts. "They always wait until you're close. They suck you in."

He's pulling at nonexistent hair.

But he's right because as I take another step toward it, the firework explodes like it should have high, high in the sky. Stars bloom at eye level, and flaming shrapnel lands on me and anyone in the first couple of rows. They stamp it out and brush it away, but it's too late. The real damage is done.

Every fuse has lit. Thirty more.

"Run!" Jamie screams and chaos ensues as fireworks go off in a variety of failures. It's a mound of fizzling, banging, light, and smoke.

Fastest, and running the farthest of all, is Uncle Jamie.

My ears ring and spots flash. A wall of hot air shoves me onto my back. Sparks spew first up into the night and then shower over me. I roll and protect my head. With another explosion, I commando crawl away, near burying myself in mud. I haul another frightened man along as I pass. Long after the final blast, an afterglow burns in my vision.

Slowly, I stand, not daring to approach the still smoking tubes. "Everyone all right?" I ask.

No one answers. People cough in the sulfurous, swirling fog.

I help a man up and spot the megaphone half-buried in the mud.

It squeals as I press the trigger to talk.

"Mud and Fire is officially over," I say. "Thank you for coming to Mud and Fire."

The first and, I suspect, the last.

Chapter 38

Despite the fireworks dud, which campers are already talking about as if it were a nuclear blast, a post-party warmth infuses the campfire tonight. The crowds from the races are gone, but more campers show than normal. We're packed in. My mother's even here, sipping her whiskey and giggling with Tina.

Four hundred and twelve. That's the number of burgers Tina sold today, nearly double Pulled Beef's record for a single day of sales. Uncle Jamie doesn't respond to mentions of the botched fireworks. He leans in close enough to the flames that no one can approach him due to the heat. He feeds the fire with his sachets, each bursting into another color with a tiny popping sound. Penny watches the colors, mesmerized. Only briefly do I wonder where Dalen is.

After my mom heads to bed, Tina joins me on my log, her hip pressing against mine as she wriggles in, fighting for a seat.

"That was awesome!" she tells me, and I realize it's the first time we've spoken since the morning.

"I can't believe you entered the race," I say.

"I know." Her eyes take on a faraway stare, a certain glassiness in them like she's had a few beers. "I don't know why I did it. Just wanted to jump off a cliff. Do something different. Know what I mean?"

There's such life in her face that it reminds me of Dalen saying to live with a little bit of vomit in the mouth. I can't think of the last time I've done something on purpose to make my stomach lurch. Except for singing to Tina.

"Dalen says that people are afraid of cliffs, not because they think they'll fall, but because they're afraid they'll jump. What you did was cool."

Penny squeals as a sachet bursts into purple fire. Uncle Jamie sighs and hands her his entire bag, brushes the dirt from his knees and turns to leave. The girl throws in another; this one flares silver. Uncle Jamie has somehow come up with new colors.

"It's magic, Mommy," Penny says.

Outside the ring of light cast by the flames, Uncle Jamie stops and stares at her.

"Penny, no," her mother says, seeing what she's playing with. "We don't play with fire."

"Please, Mommy!"

"When Mr. Saintbury comes up with a firework that doesn't need flames, you can play with them as much as you like."

A small smile touches Uncle Jamie's lips. His back straightens as he walks away.

"Tonight has a touch of magic to it, don't you think?" Tina says to me. She's close and smells of onion, wood smoke, and lemon soap. Her eyes are bright and wide, the pupils blown in the darkness. "Not even a scratch," she says, holding out her arms.

"Yeah, maybe," I say.

As if she can't help herself, Penny's mother begins flipping sachets into the fire. Everyone watches as they burst all the shades of the rainbow. Tina presses ever closer, her bare thigh against mine soon slippery with sweat. I don't care. I don't want to move. And I don't want to ask about her dad, as I worry it'll kill that magic. Whatever magic has drawn her to me tonight.

Her teeth are so white and straight. She leans in and whispers, "Would you, would you walk me back to my trailer?"

I have to cross my legs as my heart thunders. "Now?" I ask.

Her teeth tug at her bottom lip. Fingers find my hand and draw me from the log. I could be flushed from the heat, but I don't think so. No one seems to notice; they're so intent on the next sachet. As we walk hand in hand, we don't talk. I don't know Tina's excuse, but mine is that I can't.

I've kissed three girls in my life. Monica, when I was fourteen, on a dare. Lisa, when I was fifteen, at the movies—I chipped enamel from my teeth as ours clashed. Her tongue was like a light saber. And at sixteen with Steph, whom I dated for two weeks before breaking up with for the summer. Every time before a kiss, there had been this quiet, not a calm, more like the tension before an electrical storm. I know it's going to happen again when Tina stops at the muddied door of her trailer and grabs my other hand as well, pulling them to her sides, and me tight to her chest. Her eyes smile, and again I wonder if she's been drinking. Every single muscle in my body is flexed.

My fingers are sliding across her back, and hers are in my hair, gripping curls and pulling me down to her lips. It's gentle, not sloppy. Delicious without a hint of onion. I hear Penny squeal in the distance.

"Stay with me," she says. "I don't want to be here alone. Not tonight."

Again, I don't want to say anything, I don't want to break whatever spell she's under because I've never spent the night with a girl.

I kiss her harder. She giggles, and I worry that I've gone and ruined it. But instead she fumbles for the trailer key as I rub her back, not wanting to break contact. I don't remember the step, but we're on the stairs and the door is shut. I'm alone with a girl. A real one. Tina.

The RV smells of fragrant spice and a touch of incense. What did Dalen say about fragrance? *A little bit of it always clings to the hand that gives flowers.* Why am I thinking about Dalen?

Tina doesn't turn on the lights; the only illumination is from the tiny Christmas lights that encircle their screened-in porch, but still I spot the beer bottles on the table. Through the kitchen to her bedroom she leads me, bypassing the couch entirely. I can barely breathe. It's then that my mind starts to wrestle with itself. Something in all of this doesn't make sense. I like Tina. I really like her, and I want to see what it's like to be with her, and that desire is using a lot of my blood flow, but there's something in the back of my mind, telling me to slow down.

She kisses me at her bedroom door. I can't even remember what I'd been worried about as her fingernails scratch up my chest. I trace from the small of her back right up her spine to her bra strap. With a twist of my fingers the clasp comes undone and it's so fast, it must seem like I do this all the time.

"No cavorting!" Grandma yells in my brain.

"I'm sorry," I mumble between kisses. Tina places a finger to my lips, reaching under her shirt and pulling the bra free so that her breasts press out at her T-shirt. Then my hands are on them, and her hands are at my belt buckle. It's so impossibly amazing and exciting that I want to burst, and I know why they call it "getting lucky" because that's how I feel, like this wouldn't normally be happening. That's the thing I think I'm worried about.

Luck is the marriage of preparation and opportunity. I can't believe I just Dalen'ed myself. I try to clear my mind.

"You want to do this?" I ask. And I don't really care if it spoils the moment, or breaks the spell, because luck shouldn't have anything to do with sex.

"Do you have a condom?" she asks. I swallow and nod. *Always be prepared.* I don't say it's two years old. "Then, yes," she says.

Having her say it, and not leaving me to wonder, it makes it so much sweeter. Rather than guessing what I'm getting away with, I can just be.

To a mind that is still, the whole universe surrenders. Ack! More Dalen. Out, out, out!

Her shirt stretches over her head and then mine and she's hot against me. She draws farther into her room, mattress hitting the back of her knees so that she sits and takes me over top of her onto the bed. I'm breathing heavily. I taste salt on her cheek.

Tina's giving me every signal that she wants me with her tonight, but why am I not ready? Not that I'm *not* ready. I am. I *so* am. I think. That sort of readiness is making everything else so difficult to think about clearly. I recall her spinning in Pulled Beef. I picture her launching through the air in the ATV race.

The wild expression on her face, both beautiful and terrifying as she embraced Deneze. Would this be happening on any other crazy night? When her father wasn't dying alone in a hospital room? When she hasn't downed a bunch of beer? Is this just another risk she's taking? Filling her mind so as not to face reality. Am I a cliff?

"Tina," I gasp as she wrenches at the buttons of my fly like if she doesn't hurry, she'll be forced to remember. "I'm sorry," I say. "We shouldn't."

She shoves me back, not gently, and switches on the bedroom light. The spell is most definitely broken. Tears glisten in her eyes. She'd been crying already. She covers her chest. I start to say something, but she shakes her head and turns away from me.

"I want to stay, but—"

"You can go away now," she says. The light switches off.

I don't know what she's really saying. I only know what she said.

"Tina—"

"Go!"

I find my shirt on top of her bra and wait until I'm outside of her room to pull it on.

When I step out of the trailer, the shadow puppet guy's racing bears and squirrels across the side of his RV in the headlights of his car. His neighbor is watching and laughing.

Chapter 39

I wake.

It's 10:00 a.m.

I haven't slept this late in weeks. Dalen's not here, and I'm glad.

I fell asleep in my clothes. I sniff them in the hope of recapturing something from last night. But that already seems too distant. I reel from armpit stench. I could have woken next to Tina this morning. All I managed to do was push her away. I clench my hands into fists.

I have to explain what happened. At least to try. I leap from bed and step onto the concrete tile that acts as my doorstep. My hand fends off the bright sunlight filtering through the arms of branches above. A note flutters at the door. It's written on Dalen Anders, Inc. letterhead. *Come talk.*

Okay. After Tina. After chores, and priorities. I crumple the message into my pocket and head along the trail. The first thing I notice is that the road's in good shape. Shallow ruts from those trucks that left for shift this morning still run in parallel tracks, but these are normal and, with the sun out, they should stay shallow. The road's the only thing in good shape, though. That's the second thing I spot. Strewn across the entire trailer park are beer and soda cans. Burger wrappers and chip bags crinkle in the wind. How much garbage do a thousand people create in a day? Lots. Finally, the worst of it, is the mud hardening to the RVs. I glance down the road; it's not just the ones in front of me. All of them are coated on the walls facing the road.

I jog down to Tina's trailer, but she's there helping Salminder out of a taxi. His arm is over her shoulder. Gone's her flair from yesterday. Salminder looks to the muddied trailer and shakes his head at something Tina tells him. I venture no closer, but Tina glances back at me. Her eyes are cool. She gives a tiny *now's-not-the-time* shake of her head. Either that, or she hates me. I have to get to shift and hope that she'll come, too.

While Salminder faces the other way, I run past. The only clean places are the washrooms and showers, which it appears my mother has taken under her care. Somehow that annoys me more than it should. Crystal's back in her lounge chair, sullen, scratching at bug-bitten arms. But there's no bear.

On I walk, every trailer worse than the next. Several campers glance up as I pass and ask if I plan to help them with the mess I made.

"Mud races, maybe not the best idea, muh?" my mom says. She has a paintbrush in one hand and a can of white paint the other. "That driver of Dalen's been asking for you."

"Don't have time for Dalen," I mutter. I don't want to talk to anyone except Tina. "I thought you wouldn't touch the toilets?" I say. "And what's wrong with the sign as it is?"

Chips of paint flutter downward.

Her lips press. I catch the flex of her jaw muscle and then it softens. "Thought you were doing enough already," she says.

Before she replied, I already had my retort. It was a good one. *Worried I'm going to find the meaning of life in a toilet bowl?* But the look on her face isn't one I've seen very often. Once when the park had earned a little extra and she'd bought a new pump for the well. She'd had the expression then. Or when Crystal had graduated high school. And when I'd made my mom that Christmas gift, a stupid ornament that she'd treated like a crown jewel. She'd been proud.

"Well, only if you want to," I say instead.

I stop at the pool. It looks like everyone used it to clean off. Mud clouds the milky water and layers the bottom in sediment.

"Warm enough?" Penny asks from the fence.

I dip my fingers in the water. "It would be, but it's dirty."

"One more sleep, right?" she says with a sarcastic smile way, way too old for her. "I know."

I shake my head. "I think I have to empty it."

"Oh."

"I'm not going to lie to you," I say. Her eyes are disbelieving. "Not this time. I need to empty it. Clean it. Refill it, and then it's going to be cold again and it'll take time to warm. A few days in all, at least."

She looks up. "Can I help?"

"Well, yeah, if you'd like." She nods emphatically. "Meet me here tomorrow. It'll take that long to drain."

She runs off as happily as if I had told her to fetch her swimsuit and jump on in.

I connect the hose and start the process of reversing the filter

219

and pumping out the water. It spreads in a slick across the deck, flooding the smashed remains of the bears. I wonder why people destroy beautiful things.

I open the grill.

The first customer is a jack with dark circles under his eyes. He asks for a Swami Burger. When I hand it to him I say, "If you want a real future you have to focus on the present."

He looks up, eyes clearing. "What?"

"It's that Swami Burger's fortune."

He shakes his head but as he walks away, his gaze follows a bumblebee flitting between wildflowers.

To the second customer I say, "The worst thing that can happen in your life is if you never put forward that one single effort. That one chance to give something everything you've got and see what happens."

It's a skinny rail of a man. He squints at me. "Says who?"

"Someone on the Internet," I say, and then think, *and probably Dalen, too.*

"The cost of being awesome is taking responsibility for your thoughts," I say to a woman.

"I think you're losing it," she says with a wink, and then cocks her head as if trying to recollect something, "Every challenge is an opportunity."

"Ha, good one," I say. "Mine was Churchill, sort of." I hear giggling. Penny lifts the pool hose and lets it shower down on her as the pool empties. *Every challenge is an opportunity.* "A really good one," I say to the woman's back.

Between customers, I run back to the pool and shut off the pump.

To Penny's dismay, I explain, "Can you tell campers that they can hose down their RVs at the pool, please?" She looks downcast until I add, "You can help, if you want to."

Again she sprints off as if I was paying her in candy.

The pool has only gone down an inch or two. Plenty of water remains to wash down all the muddied trailers, solving two problems at once. Minutes later, Penny returns, leading the first trailer. I have a broom from Pulled Beef that works well on the dirty siding without scratching it. Only one side of every RV is covered, so it takes less time than I'd have thought and almost everyone buys a burger while they clean, with Penny gleefully directing the hose.

Today starts to look up, but between the washing and grill I don't have a chance to deal with the garbage, and I worry about the bears. The worst part is, Tina fails to show for her shift. I lock up alone and head, exhausted, to rebuild the campfire from last night. I search for scrap paper to act as a wick to start the fire and find the note from Dalen in my pocket and realize I haven't seen him all day.

That's when Grandma starts to move.

Chapter 40

"Hey, where you taking Grandma?" I shout.

Mom's there with Deneze and a couple of his friends. The extension cord hangs unplugged down the statue's back. The generators have been left behind at the original site.

"Don't worry, we'll get 'er plugged back in," Mom says. Grandma's brain is tucked underneath her arm.

"But why are you moving her?" I ask. "It's not what she wanted."

"Boy, I've lived under that woman's shadow for fifty years, and I'm not gonna live there another day."

Deneze stands, waiting as we talk.

"Where are you taking her?" I ask.

"It's time to put her in the corner." She points to the edge of the campground.

"Was she really so nasty?" I ask.

"Over there." My mom directs Deneze and his crew and then turns back to me. "Nasty? No, she was a friggin' saint."

I can't tell if it's sarcasm as she hurries to catch up. Grandma's brain sloshes about in the container.

"Uncle Jamie okay with this?" I shout.

"She was *my* mother," she shouts back.

"Well . . . it's my statue," I yell. "For now."

Her hands press at her hips as she glares. "Ray, this one's not about you."

She turns away.

"Put her facing the Big at least," I reply.

She doesn't look back, but she holds a thumb in the air. "And don't forget to plug her into the park grid!" I shout.

I cringe when I hear the release of compressed gas. It's the bus door opening. I've been avoiding talking to Dalen. Not only did he flub his performance yesterday, but I still wonder if there's anything he's told me I couldn't have read out of a book or off a bunch of quotes on a webpage somewhere.

With the fire set, I hesitate, not looking forward to a conversation with Dalen. I have lots to do though and fill what remains of my day with garbage hauling and RV cleaning. But I can't avoid the bus door that whooshes open every time I pass within sight. Finally, I walk over to the bus steps. Charlie's in her seat. "Hi, Dalen here?" I ask.

"Out for a walk."

I glance down the road. "Said he wanted to talk to me."

"That was me," she says. "Get in."

I do, and the door shuts behind me. She stands. With the door shut and me at the bottom of the stairwell, I'm surrounded with nowhere to look but up at her.

"Dalen's been on a walk since this morning," she says.

"It's not my fault he—"

Charlie holds up a hand.

"You know what? We all have fault in everything. We're all cogs in everyone else's wheel. Heck, it's my fault that some kid's being run over a thousand miles from here. I probably could be there if I'd made different choices in life, but I'm not, so let's focus on the here and now, all right?"

I blink.

"Good. Now yesterday you asked Dalen if anything he said was his. Not regurgitated dogma." My cheeks heat. "I can't answer that question," she says. "I drive the bus. But I bet Dalen can."

"So what's the matter?"

Charlie drew a deep breath as if she wasn't sure she should say anything more. "You're important to Dalen. He has a daughter, you know?"

I nod.

"You were a chance to have a part of that relationship back. When he first started out, Dalen worked with people in small towns, with real problems. Divorces, addictions, he made a difference to individuals. Helped me, too. Then those towns became stops on a book tour. A really, really successful book tour, and his job became less about listening and more about selling books and speeches. Do you understand?"

"No," I say. "He knows everyone here. Better than I do. My mom's out there, moving Grandma and painting the gate, and I don't think she would be if all this hadn't happened."

Charlie's nodding her head. "That's what I mean! Here, he's different. He's not coddling rock stars or helping CEOs schedule quality time with their kids. He's back to the essence of things, individuals, not crowds. He was loving it."

"Until yesterday," I say.

"He stepped out yesterday, slipped back into celebrity sales mode."

"And failed."

"It was a slip," she corrects.

"But he says that if you're not failing, if you're not embarrassing yourself, then you're not trying hard—"

Charlie's waving her hands like an umpire signaling *safe*. "Saying and doing, very different."

"What do you need from me?" I ask.

The windows darken as the sun cuts low over the forest.

"Just don't give up on him, okay? Give him a chance."

I can see the pain in her eyes. The empathy. I realize that if I'd felt that kind of shared pain for Tina, I wouldn't have even considered sleeping with her last night; we never would have made it near the bedroom.

"Don't give up on him," she says. "He hasn't on you." Charlie hands down a check.

"What's this for?" I ask. It's written out to Salminder. Just over ten thousand dollars.

"The news release Dalen sent, it was as a fundraiser for Salminder to help him through his treatments. Dalen matched every donation, to the penny."

Unbidden, tears flood my eyes, and I climb the stairs to hug her.

"Thank you," I say, but I know words alone are not enough. Some fixing requires doing.

Chapter 41

I'm wringing my hands as I approach Salminder's trailer. The check's in my sweaty hand, but I'm not nervous about that. The last time I was here, I was groping his daughter.

I knock on a post of the screened-in area. Salminder waves from his lawn chair.

"Welcome back." He's pale, lost more weight, and I realize now how I missed his comment weeks ago about being on a terrible diet. Yeah, a cancer diet. If I'd been looking, I could have seen the signs. His skin sags, and the total lack of hair on his body is still strange.

"I hear the Swami Burger's a top seller. I need to get sick more often," he says, and there's a rasp to his voice that hadn't been there.

"I'd rather we sell less and you get better," I say. "Maybe this will help. It's from Dalen, and Mud and Fire."

I hand him the check. His eyes water before clearing again. "Getting sick can be profitable, who knew?" he says. "My secret is out, then."

"Sorry, Dalen didn't tell me that . . . I mean . . . I'm sorry, I told him."

We're silent for a minute. It's not quite the reaction I'd expected.

"Where is he so I can thank him?" Salminder asks.

"He's off for a walk, a long one. I think I've driven him away. I was really angry with him and asked if anything that came out of his mouth was his. He really bombed yesterday."

"And after he bombed, what did you do?"

I lower my chin. "Nothing." Worse than nothing. I avoided him, but my thoughts—those had been *so* negative and *so* mean.

"Nothing." Even with the waggly skin, Salminder's jaw sets. "Of this I am sure: that the man my daughter will choose to be with will be a *good* man."

"What?" I lean forward, knuckles white on the arms of the chair. "You mean me? I never said I . . ."

Of course, he's heard about last night. There are no secrets in an RV park. And then there *was* the serenading.

"You may not know it, but I know. I know." His eyes fill with life, but I'd rather not have all their fire focused on me. "Are you a good man, Raymond?"

"I think so," I say without conviction.

"You can return and speak to my daughter only when you know so."

"When I know the meaning of life, you mean?" I ask with a sad laugh. After all that's happened I don't feel any closer. "How am I supposed to do that?"

He struggles to sit up in the lounge chair.

"Son . . ."

Son. It's such a simple word, but it's not one I've ever heard from a man. And of all men, he's the only one I want to hear it from.

"How?" My throat's tight with emotion.

"Don't eat crap," he says.

"Food?" I ask.

"Yes, food. But not only food. Learn something every day. Think about what you can do better the next day. Don't talk so much. Exercise more. Listen to good music. Learn to appreciate the beauty around you. Believe in yourself, no one else can quite as fiercely. Live simply.

"Build this." He taps his head. "Everything else will follow. A million dollars does nothing for the soul."

"Nothing else? That's it?" It and so much at the same time.

"Through my eyes I remember beauty and give it meaning. I give the grass meaning by feeling it between my toes. The starlings who fight off the crow, by protecting my own. By witnessing life, I give it meaning."

I frown; sometimes I want to punch the meaning of life in the head. Maybe there's an easier way to force a clear answer. "That's what it means to be Sikh?"

His fingers trace his turban. "A Sikh's life is of humble service, service without expectation of return."

"Why isn't Tina religious?"

"She doesn't find meaning in it."

"That's okay?"

"It is. Belief without meaning is a lie."

I pause. Trying to combine everything I've heard from Dalen, from Salminder, but it's still not clear. "What would you do with a million dollars?" I ask.

"Really, boy? Who says I don't already have a million dollars? Stop assuming. Trust your gut. I believe in you."

Salminder's a trailer-park millionaire? "Grandma believed in me. Enough to write it into a will. I've only known her as a crotchety, ancient woman who sometimes came to my defense. How'd she know to believe in me? The gaming? Was it the wood chopping? Was that some sort of crazy test, moving my hand before it was chopped off?"

"She was old when I came here, too, but maybe she saw some of her younger self in you."

"Really? That's a good thing?"

"I wasn't here at the time, but I heard about it. Your grandma had been a nurse. Her husband died at forty-five from a heart attack. She'd been working hard, late shifts, never around for the kids, and his death had been a wake-up call. She bought land after he died and opened the campground to anyone else who needed a retreat like she did at the time. I'm not sure she knew what she was doing. She was a mess. Those who took her up on it weren't in need of only peace, however; they wanted homes, and so your grandma pulled from the back forties of local farms old, rotting trailers. That first summer five women slept here. That number would grow to dozens."

Those signatures on the trailers, I realize, they're not from just any campers. Most of them are from people Grandma helped.

I'm stunned. I'm so stunned that I don't move when Tina slips out of the trailer and walks past us toward the washrooms.

Salminder's head seems loose on his neck. His eyelids droop. I should leave and let him rest, but I have one more question.

"What happened? Why did she turn it into an RV park?" I ask.

"You arrived. And your sister. Your mom needed help, and they needed money."

Grandma *was* a saint, at least for a bit. A shadow that my mother could never climb out from under.

I thank the dozy Salminder and try to catch up with Tina. But she's too far ahead and disappears into the washroom. I'm pretty sure it would be creepy to stalk her by waiting outside, and even creepier to actually go inside, so I change direction and head to the fire.

Uncle Jamie's there and he's grinning as though he has a secret. He holds out a bag of his sachets to Penny. Her mother rises from her log and frowns at him.

"I said no playing with fire, Mr. Saintbury."

He nods. "I know. Go on."

Penny looks to her mother. "They're safe?" she asks.

He reaches inside and pulls out a tiny bag. These are packed tighter and smaller; there's a twist of paper at the top, and they remind me of Hershey's Kisses. He's dyed each package what I suspect is the same color as the flare. Instead of tossing it in the fire, he throws one into the air and holds out his palm. The packet lands dead center and bursts lime green with a violent snap. He shakes out his hand, but he's smiling.

Penny whoops, and she reaches out even as she looks up to her mother. She sighs her acquiescence.

The girl picks through the colors and starts setting them off one after the other, dropping them at her feet.

She giggles. "It's like . . . like *unicorn farts.*"

Her mother gasps. "Penny!" But then she covers her mouth and laughs along.

"That's it," Jamie says with one fist punched in the air. "Grandma's Unicorn Farts. It's perfect."

He runs off as if he needs to write it down, and I'm left wondering what Grandma had to do with any of this. I'm smiling when I look up to see Charlie, mouth pursed with worry.

"Dalen's not back yet, is he?" I ask.

She shakes her head. "I'm worried, Ray. He might be lost." She clutches her elbows, chilled on a warm night.

I see the unspoken question.

Are you a good man, Raymond? But it's dark. Very dark.

Chapter 42

"It's too late," my mom says.

"It's late for Dalen, too," I reply.

Tina's arrived, helping Salminder to sit on the log.

"We don't want more people lost," Salminder says.

Charlie is still looking at me.

"Crystal," I shout.

She comes out of the office trailer and stands in a nightgown. "What?"

"Dalen's lost in the woods," I explain.

"It's too dark," she says and turns back around.

"Do you have lights?" I ask.

"Of course I have lights, but it is too late and too dark to go out after him now. Do you even know where he started?" she demands, and I look at Charlie, who shrugs. "Then how are we going to track him in the dark? If he's unconscious somewhere, you could hike by him all night and never see a thing."

Everyone looks to me now.

"Don't we have to try?" I ask.

I peer beyond the campfire light, but the woods are a moat of darkness. The fire's warm, the lethargic heat radiating from deep orange coals. Coals perfect for marshmallow roasting. For ghost stories of naïve campers lost in the woods.

"It's only been since when? Morning?" Obelix says.

"Not supposed to be cold or to rain tonight," Penny's mother says. "He shouldn't get hypothermia if we wait."

Shouldn't. This isn't about Dalen. It's about protecting me.

"I'm scared," Penny replies.

It might not be raining, but the swamp's wet. I'm terrified of the thought of entering the bush at night. I am happy to be talked out of this. With the clouds it's nearly pitch black. Why would he run off into the woods?

Because I accused him of being a fraud . . .

Tina moves forward to me and whispers, "What about the bear?"

I can feel the blood run from my face. I'd forgotten about that.

Crystal wanders closer.

"What was he wearing?" I ask Charlie.

"Shorts and a T-shirt."

"So Dalen is freezing, probably soaked through in the swamp, and likely being eaten by a bear." No one corrects me. Wet, bear, my fault. It's Grandma all over again. My video game. My fireball. "That's it, I'm going."

"You can have my gun," Obelix says. "I think I'd only slow you down."

Penny hugs her mother. Tina stands by her dad. She's not coming.

"I'll come," Charlie says.

"And me," Crystal grumbles, stepping into the light. "No way I'm letting you shoot my bear. Yer always stealing crap from me."

"What?" I ask.

"You, yer always getting everything for doing nothing," she snaps.

"What are you talking about?"

"Just shut it, all right?"

Obelix breathes heavily as he returns from his trailer to hand me the big revolver.

"Loaded," he says and gives me the holster for it. The belt's so big I loop it over my shoulder.

"Just don't be firing that near me," Crystal says and huffs off, hem of her dressing gown wafting. When she returns she's changed and carries two rifles, one a high-powered gun, the second her .22, which might tickle the bear, but won't slow it down any. She hands that one to Charlie, who holds it with her arms out at full extension.

"Not loaded," Crystal says. "Go get some boots, flashlight, food and water. Don't just stand around." My mother's following all this with a strange grin. Crystal shouts at me, "You, too. Go!"

I run back to my trailer, gun slapping at my stomach. I pull a knapsack from under the bed, cough at the litter of dust bunnies that comes with it, and search in my fridge for something to eat. Half a stick of butter. I drink what is left in the plastic milk jug and fill it with water before stuffing a headlamp, matches, and rope inside. The straps bite at my shoulders, but the weight will lessen as I drink the water.

Back at the fire, Charlie's wearing a pair of designer hiking boots and a Canada Goose parka. At least she'll be warm. "Let's go," I say, and I feel good. *Really good.* Like I have purpose.

Everyone wishes us luck. Mother squelches a radio, and it seems to remind Crystal to hand me one. "We're on channel six."

I've used these before and swing its holster around my other shoulder. At the edge of the firelight, I hesitate.

"Come on, cowboy," Crystal says, and I step into darkness.

I switch on my headlamp and draw a deep breath in its white light. The mosquitoes have dwindled in the late hour. We return to the bus. From there Crystal scans the ground for tracks, skirting the shoulder of the road and the fringe of swampy woods. Eventually she shrugs and starts in.

"Did you see something?" I ask.

"No," Crystal says.

"Then why are we going this way."

"Lived here all your life and never been in Grandma's bush, have you?"

Charlie cocks her head at me.

"It's wet in Grandma's bush," I say.

"Parts of her bush are dry," Crystal replies.

Charlie covers her mouth with her palm.

"What's so funny about Grandma's bush?" Crystal asks.

I snort.

"Don't be gross." Crystal shakes her head, but there's a smile on her face as she marches farther into the woods.

"Why are we going this way?" I ask again. The last time I hiked this far into the swamp I met a pack of wolves.

"Because everyone goes this way."

"How—"

"Because it's toward Big, you watch. Anyone leaving camp for a hike heads toward Big. Why? Because it's there. Besides there's a hump here, can take us through the swamp dry."

"But—"

"I brought two radios for a reason. A half mile in this trail splits. If we don't see tracks, then . . ." She leaves it unsaid with a wink. She knows the dark's a problem for me. She's enjoying this.

"How much food you got?" she asks.

"Huge jug of water," I say.

She stops short. "Nothing to eat? You idiot. And what about you?"

Charlie turns to show her pack. "Power Bars. Whole box of them. Strawberry flavor. No water though."

"Yer not even ready for a yoga class." Then Crystal curls her hand around her mouth. "Dalen!" We all jump. "What, we're not sneaking up on the guy, are we?" Crystal asks.

"Sorry," I reply. "You're right."

Between calls we walk in silence, listening. Only the *woot, woot, woot, wooooot* of a barred owl replies to our shouts. Charlie wanders off path and swears at a soaker.

My mind begins to run back to the campfire and the twist of hatred I'd caught on Crystal's lips. "What did you mean when you said, I get everything?" I ask her.

Crystal sniffs. "Listen, I don' wanna get into this."

"Come on, it's obvious Mom likes you best, how do *I* get everything? I get nothing."

An argument's a welcome distraction from the curtains of

shadows that seem to shift and grab. Crystal tromps a few more steps before responding.

"Which is why I've spent five years cleaning toilets?"

"At least you have someone to talk to."

"You have yer gaming geeks."

"It's not my fault."

"Well, it's sure not mine neither." She shakes her head. "You're the one with a chance at a million."

"This is about the money?" I ask.

"Yes, it's about the money." *Thump, thump, thump.* I'm pretty sure it's my imaginary head she's squashing beneath her boots. "Grandma said it was too late for me already. You remember that in the will?"

"I didn't ask for the money and, you know, maybe Grandma shouldn't be listened to."

She's silent for a moment. Charlie has fallen back a few steps as if to let us hash this out.

"It's about how Mama never made you do nothing," Crystal continues. "About how my college money went to your hockey practices that you did nothing with. About how you get a trailer and I get nothing. About how you get money from Salminder and I get nothing."

"What?" I halt, but she keeps trudging. "Mom *made* me do hockey. And she's not forcing you to stay anymore. You've got three options. Leave. Change the situation. Or accept it." I jog to catch up.

Crystal's silent, this time for a minute and then says, "I don't know what to do, Ray, I seriously don't."

I swallow, realizing that she's really asking me. "When are you happy?" I ask.

She rolls her eyes, but answers anyways, "Hunting."

"Why hunting?"

Her face reddens under the light of my headlamp.

"Because I get superpowers."

"Oh," I say.

"You don't get it. In here, I am in control. I can feed myself for weeks. I can make a lean-to, dig myself in, start fires with sticks. And it's like my eyesight sharpens, hearing too, even smell sometimes, like I'm this alpha-predator."

"Alpha-predator," I repeat.

"Yeah."

There's a distant look on her face. It's an expression I've seen on Dalen. Crystal, I realize, is enlightened when she is hunting. She's present. She's aware of everything, and not thinking about the past or the future. At peace, with a gun in her hand.

"That's why you stay," I say. "Figure out a way to hunt more."

"Whatcha mean?"

"You stay because this is your home. If you left and got some job in town bagging groceries or something, you wouldn't be able to hunt. Not as much."

She stops, pushes out her lips in thought and says, "Yep. That's part sure."

Then she keeps walking.

"That's it? I figure out your meaning of life and all you say is, yep?"

"You're still a twerp." I'm about to say something more, but she holds up her hand. We halt. "We're here."

Sure enough, the birch trees that grow away from the water

lead off in two prongs of a ghostly fork.

"It'll be okay," Charlie says with a hand at my shoulder.

I'd been shaking my head and not even realizing it.

I shout for Dalen, but . . . nothing.

"Fear is nothing to be afraid of. Letting it control you is the problem," Crystal says. "Or so I hear."

I frown. "Salminder said that."

"Nope, Dalen. I'm sure of it."

Huh.

"Charlie," Crystal says. "You ever fire a gun?" Charlie shakes her head. "Then yer with me."

"You're leaving me alone?" I ask and hate how my voice cracks.

Crystal hands me the .22. "You won't hit a damn thing with that big handgun. Take this. The .22's a varmint gun, but it can do the job of a more powerful gun if you aim right."

The circle of light cast by my headlamp makes the darkness beyond darker. Crystal nudges Charlie down her stretch of path.

My pulse quickens as I walk down my path, alone.

The radio squelches. "Good luck, little brother."

Next time I hear her, she's calling for Dalen. She sounds so far away.

Chapter 43

I made a few mistakes back at the fork in the trail. I didn't get more batteries, and the light of my headlamp has gone sallow and, although I'm not thirsty, I'm really hungry. I'd even eat a strawberry Power Bar, but they're filling Charlie's pack, not mine.

A branch cracks, and I whirl. But the weak light can't penetrate far enough. "My headlamp's almost out," I say into the radio.

"Dark don't kill," Crystal replies.

The light fails. Immediately I forget which way I'm facing. Darkness envelops me. Had I whirled to the right, or to the left? Another snap and I hold my breath. Something skitters up a tree. "Probably a squirrel," I say to myself. Everything sounds louder in the dark. "Light's out," I speak into the radio.

"Geez, jes wait for yer eyes to adjust."

I double squelch back. The sound's loud in the swamp-dampened woods, but night rushes back in.

Crystal's right. There's not much light, only a fog of it fighting through the clouds, but the darkness isn't complete.

Soon I make out birch trees, then the black pines beyond. I might even be able to see farther now than with the light.

A coyote howls, its call answered in the distance. "Coyote, you sure that's a coyote?" I ask the radio.

I flash back to the tracking wolves and shake it off.

"It's the bear you should be worried about."

"Thanks, thanks a lot, sis." I start forward and drop into mud. Water seeps over the tops of my boots as I first wrestle one boot out of the muck and then topple free of the second, bare foot in the air. I flounder for the buried boot, but it's already covered in water. I feel for it, fingers tracing roots and twigs, something slimy, and finally a lace. I pull, and the boot comes up slowly. Finally, it yanks free.

I'm grateful for the darkness. I scrape the worst of the mud off and shake out the water, before pulling on the soaked sock and then the boot. It's wet and cold and weighs five pounds more, but it reminds me that somewhere out here Dalen's lost, perhaps hurt.

I squelch on. Still jolting at every sound. The darkness magnifies it, or perhaps it's because I've never really listened this hard. Crystal's superpowers.

I freeze mid-eye roll.

Something snuffles.

"Dalen!" I shout. For a second, as the call echoes from Big, the snuffling stops. But then it comes back.

Closer.

I back up a few steps, my heel pressing into softer earth. I edge along the swamp, deeper into the forest. A twig breaks. Maybe it was a branch. I fight the urge to run.

I unshoulder the gun. Open the chamber and try to plug in a cartridge, dropping several before I get one in. The others are lost to rich earth. "It's okay, Ray, not like there's a man-eating bear out here," I mutter under my breath. "Oh yeah, there is."

Snap.

Definitely a branch. There are few forest creatures big enough to split a branch. I clench my eyes shut and remind myself that I once thought a squirrel on top of my trailer was a man with a hook for a hand, opening the roof like a tin can.

Snuffle, snuffle.

I start to run. Behind me are definite steps. Grumbles. This is why I'm afraid of the dark. I feel for the radio. "Bear, bear," I squeak. My throat tight with fear.

"My bear!" Crystal shouts back.

"I don' . . . care . . . whose . . . bear . . ."

"Don't run. We are coming. Try to shoot it."

There's no running from a bear. I force myself to stop as I watch the dark shape thirty feet back along the trail. That grizzly should be chewing on me.

"Shoot it!" Crystal says at the same time as Charlie shouts, "No!"

Bears are fast. You're not supposed to run. You're not supposed to climb trees; bears can climb faster. Even a grizzly might shimmy after you up a tree. If this one's been stalking me, that means this isn't a defensive attack, it's predatory. It means to eat me. A .22 is not a high-caliber bullet; it's enough to seriously piss off a bear in the wrong spot. Kill it in the perfect one. What the rifle doesn't have is stopping power. But right now it's all I've got.

I lift my arms and make myself big.

"Hey there! Hey you! Go away!"

It stands. I bring the rifle to my shoulder. This isn't the first time I've fired a gun, and I don't mean in a video game. My sister and I used to knock cans off posts as targets. Sometimes during the late fall and early spring there really isn't much else to do in the evenings. So I'm a decent shot. I can hit this black shadow.

But something's not quite right. There's no eye shine. No yellow-orange reflection of the dim moonlight. My finger hovers over the trigger. The bear's too small. This isn't the bear that hugged Grandma.

"It's Dalen," the radio crackles with Charlie's warning. "The bear's Dalen."

"Dalen?" I ask.

The sudden light of his headlamp shines out of the darkness, and I swing the barrel away.

"You were going to shoot me?" Dalen asks.

"You were a bear."

"I'm not," he gasps.

"Why didn't you say anything, I was calling, and . . . wait . . ." I squint at him. He's dressed in black, a heavy sweater and pants. Good army-style boots, and he's wearing a pack that's full. "Why did Charlie know you weren't a bear?"

He starts toward me.

"No, stop," I say, backing up a few steps. "What is this?"

"You faced your greatest fear," he says.

"It was a trick," I whisper. I'm cold, hungry, and tired. Now add angry. "I think I'm going to kill you anyways."

Chapter 44

"Too many people let fear stop them from achieving their dreams," Dalen says.

"Who said that?" I ask, "Jesus? Martin Luther King? Winston Churchill? No, I've got it. It's an ancient Chinese proverb, isn't it?" This pushes Dalen into silence. "Seriously, I bet I could program you into an Instagram profile, every hour a new missive from the past."

I heave with deep breaths. I quake with cold and spent fear.

"What ideas are mine?" Dalen asks. "It's a fair question, not the best timed, but fair. There's a good answer, though, and that is if I see farther than others, it's only because I stand on the shoulders of those wiser than myself. There's nothing wrong with that. No teacher relies on what they figure out themselves. Wisdom is wisdom. Second-hand wisdom is like second-hand gold. It holds whatever value is ascribed by its holder."

I turn away and start hiking back toward Sunny Days. The rhetoric all sounds the same—fool's gold. There's a dark shape ahead, darker than the rest of the night, and I'm surprised that Crystal and Charlie made it back so quickly.

"Ray, did you conquer your fear of the dark tonight?"

I keep walking; the light from his headlamp has ruined my night vision, so that I zigzag over the trail from swamp to swamp.

"We're on our way back," Crystal says in the radio. "I didn't know."

I peer into the darkness again, searching for the shape, but I can't make anything out now that I've left the area lit by Dalen's headlamp.

"If you get to camp early, Charlie," I respond to the radio, "you can start packing up."

"What do you fear, Ray?" Dalen asks to my back. "What are you hiding from?"

"You're a circus act."

Our boots make sucking sounds as we trod in silence for a bit. Every time I think I hear something in the swamp, Dalen speaks, covering the sound.

"I have been a circus act," Dalen agrees. "Yesterday, for instance. Today, I'm not. I'm choosing today. What are you choosing? Why are you hiding from yourself?"

"Look at me," I scoff. Bugs swarm my ears. It's as if their angry buzz has entered my brain, and they distract me from what could be in the woods. "My journey's starting with each step. And . . . and . . . I know where I'm going, so I know how to get there." My words are bitter. In my tone, I hear my mother at her worst.

"You can fire me. But you are not the first person I have tried to help. You do not like all of my methods, but consider it all together. I invite you to have faith that I have something to offer, help that is worth having."

"Fine. Hundred thousand dollar man, you have the walk to camp," I say.

He seems to consider this. He's behind me, and he wrestles with a sapling I purposefully let swing back in his face.

"Okay, answer my questions, though. I asked you a question, Ray. Have you faced your fear of the dark?"

"Yeah, now I'm just afraid of bears." I start hiking faster.

"What's changed at the park? Be honest with yourself," he says.

I don't say anything. All I can think is that Tina had liked me and now she doesn't. How I'd thought I wanted to be a pro gamer, but the way followers keep leaving me . . .

"Let's start with something I noticed yesterday. How about the shadow-puppet man. He's now friends with his neighbor."

"Hardly big," I say.

"Friendship? Not big?" He hustles to catch up. "Fine though, the little girl hasn't asked about the pool lately, has she?"

"Given up."

"No, she doesn't need it. The pool was a distraction from what she was missing. She needs a community and she has that now."

"I'm still going to clean it," I say.

"Your mother has taken ownership of the park. She's moving out from under your grandma's wing. She's realized her meaning."

I can't argue with that one. "It's not her park yet."

"What about Jamie? He believes in Grandma's Unicorn Farts." The only way Dalen could know these things is if Charlie's been in contact with Dalen all day. My mood darkens. "And Obelix?"

He's pretty happy. There it goes again. The sucking sounds of slow steps in swamp water.

"What about your sister? Anything change for her?" I shrug, half-listening. "What are the happiest moments of this week?"

I picture Tina pulling off her helmet. That was the best one, but there were others. Penny and the berg. Uncle's magic. My mom smiling at me. Really smiling.

Dalen must see it on my face because he says, "You did this."

"No."

"You did. You created the environment for it. By helping others find their meaning, your life will have meaning too. When you mix things up, stuff happens. You have to learn to trust in that, to step out and just see what happens. Fear of change is often the biggest cliff to leap from. Tonight, you conquered fear."

"I faced down an old insane man, that's all." I stop as a cold chill runs over me. It prickles like the thawing of skin after diving into the icy pool. Things may have changed. Dalen may be right. But I don't see the formula. My family and other campers may be happier, but most of it happened just because. I didn't do it on purpose. Tina was the only one I intended to make happy, and since I've been working with Dalen she's become more miserable. "I'm not going to find the meaning of life in time, am I?"

"It sounds to me like ever since you started this quest, everything's changed. You say you're not any closer to finding meaning, but everyone else is. So why not you?"

I stop and hang my head. "Tina, she hates me."

His hand grips my shoulder. I listen to crickets and the rustling of the dark. *Heavy* rustling.

"I honestly don't know what passed between you. Whatever it is is too painful to discuss. I am sorry it did." The sincerity makes my chest ache. "Sometimes when people are wrong it's hard to hear it from someone close to them. Grief is a difficult emotion."

"Gandhi?" I ask.

"All me. And here's another one. Apologize—it clears closets."

"What if I don't know what I'm apologizing for?"

"It's never all your fault. We all make mistakes. Admit your part in them and move on. Here's the secret. You say, 'I'm sorry.' It may feel like your share in the fault is small and it's much greater for the other person. But you can't accurately measure fault; luckily apologies don't care who did what, and they cost nothing. That's all mine too. Or maybe it's not. Who knows? But, speaking of me, I've decided to go back to my roots."

"Book tour?" I joke.

"Something like that." He chuckles. "So, do you still think I'm just spouting proverbs and quotes—" The word quotes comes out strangled with emotion, and I'm touched that my opinion means so much to him.

I turn to face Dalen, but his eyes are wide and glaring over my shoulder. Something snorts. "There's a bear, isn't there?" I ask. His nod's barely perceptible. "Close?"

"Here."

Hot breath rolls over my neck.

Chapter 45

"Don't run," I whimper.

I hear the pop of the bear's jaw and then blowing and snorting. I cringe. But there's no playing dead with a bear this close. Not one that's trailed us. Crystal taught me that. The only hope is to fight. But it's a bear. A grizzly. And it's *so* dark.

Dalen's wrong. I didn't conquer my fear. When I'd thought he was the bear, my first reaction had been to run. If he had been a bear, I would have been dead. Dalen's words haven't changed anything for me, but they have given me a spark of desire.

Into my mind comes Tina, our banter, her drive to be more, her wild smile. I need to see her. I have to make things right. But there's this grizzly in my way.

I turn and the bear lifts on barrel legs. Yellow jaws roar at the sky. There isn't even room to swing the rifle. I-can-not-run. A long string of drool dangles from the bear's muzzle and catches me across the cheek. It reeks of garbage and carrion, its last meal. Me—its next.

I raise my arms and bellow, the snarl burning my throat.

But Dalen runs.

It's a mistake. There's no escape. I manage to give the bear a glancing blow on the thick furred neck with the rifle butt, but it's nothing. It swats at me with a paw, a rake of claws that catches my hip and flings me into the swamp. As I fly through the air, all I can do is struggle to keep the gun out of the water.

I land against a felled tree trunk. The pain sends glowing spots into my vision. I don't know how injured I am. My mind's numb and blank. My thigh feels hot as the rest of me cools. Dalen's light jogs about fifty yards off. It illuminates the pawing grizzly, claws swinging at something up in a tree that hollers. I worm out of the swamp, keeping the gun out of the muck, and climb to unsteady feet.

Now I can run. But I know I can't. Old-Ray might have panicked and scrambled in the opposite direction, but Better-Ray stays. I lift the rifle to my shoulder.

With the bear sighted, I fire. The short recoil nudges me back. I jerked the trigger, pulling up on the barrel and missing the bear, which has begun to test its weight on the trunk. The tree whipsaws.

Dalen screams. "You shot me! I've been shot! You shot me!"

"Sorry!" I fumble in my pocket for another round. It's a bolt-action rifle and only takes one shot at a time. I find a round, knock out the spent casing and slip this one in, easing closer to the bear.

Dalen keeps shouting, which I take to mean he's not dying straight away.

I take aim. Draw a deep, slow breath the way my mother and Crystal showed me. I squeeze the trigger.

This time the rifle shot cracks thunderously. It's as if the bear's been stung. It swats at its head, topples to the side, and kicks twice before lying still.

"Always trying to take what's mine," Crystal says from behind me.

I turn and see her lower her gun.

"Sorry, I had to," I say.

"Sorry for what?"

"Killing the bear."

"Check your weapon, bro," she says.

I do. The bullet is still in the chamber. Crystal got her bear.

From above comes cracking and the sound of branches giving. Dalen falls out of the tree. He lands with a whump on top of the grizzly, screeches, and rolls away.

"Dalen!" Charlie sprints for him, falling to her knees.

"I'm sorry, I'm sorry," I say as I run forward and take the opposite side. Dalen's eyes are clenched tight. "I don't think you're a fraud, I don't, I don't, I'm just an idiot. I'll answer your questions. I will. What do I fear? What do I fear? I fear I'll make the wrong choices. I fear I've wasted all this time doing nothing, avoiding doing something. I'm afraid that if I admit that, all that time goes up in smoke, like paff."

"Paff? This is still all about you?" Crystal demands to know. "You shot him and you're talking about you." She's got her gun trained on the bear; she's smart like that.

Dalen's grimacing, but I can tell it's only partly due to the pain; the rest is all grin.

"You needed to shoot me to get to the truth? It'll cost extra." He chuckles and grips the side of his leg. His hand is oily red. "It's not too bad, think I can walk."

"That's because you were just shot. In thirty minutes it's going to hurt like hell. Unless you go into shock." Crystal tosses me her pack. "First aid." I look back at her. "I'm not saying take the bullet out, just take his pants off and bind his leg."

I nod and help Dalen shimmy out of his pants.

"Shouldn't have run, I guess," Dalen says.

"Probably saved me," I reply.

"You challenged the bear." There's real amazement in Dalen's eyes. "Stood up to a monster in the dark. That's not average, Better-Ray—I know."

When we get his pants off, Charlie pours some hydrogen peroxide over it, cleansing the wound. Blood continues to trickle down his leg.

I bind it.

I can tell Crystal's right; it hasn't been thirty minutes, but the pain's starting to settle into the creases on his face.

"Mom," Crystal speaks into the radio. "We've a gunshot wound to the thigh, .22 at forty yards."

"They'll survive," Mom replies, but her voice shakes. "That was dumb. Is it Ray?"

"Really?" I say.

"Dalen's shot. Ray shot him. We'll need an ambulance," Crystal says.

"I was aiming for the bear," I shout.

"Air?" my mom asks.

Crystal looks to Dalen. "You want an air lift? Costs a mint."

"Yep," Dalen says between clenched teeth.

"Air," Crystal says. "They can't land here, so send an ATV in to pick him up."

There's a double squelch in reply.

Crystal props up Dalen's legs and removes a blanket from her bag to cover him. I see now that he's shuddering despite the relatively warm night.

Charlie keeps waving mosquitoes off of Dalen's pallid face with no concern for herself.

I wipe his blood on my jeans.

"I'm sorry," I say again.

"You were shooting at the bear," Charlie says.

"He's usually a better shot," Crystal replies.

There is a distant sound of the ATV. A steady faraway buzz, but it'll be slow going with the swamp and the trees.

"I don't want you to go, Dalen. I'm sorry." His breathing's shallow and tight and he holds as still as possible. "You're not fired."

"Ray, you've got this one," he says through clenched teeth.

"But I don't, I don't know it."

We all know what *it* is.

"Pretty sure you do, kid. You're above average and all."

I'm out of time and now that it's gone, I feel as though I've wasted so much of it. The ATV's lights rip along the strip of dry land, weaving around trees, and then it rumbles to a stop where Crystal's flashing her headlamp. Uncle Jamie's driving and he's all business, helping to carry Dalen to the seat.

Charlie props him up in the ATV, sitting behind him, leaving me with my sister.

Crystal's eyes are narrowed at me. She grips the long rifle by the barrel, its butt on her boot toe as we watch the ATV drive away.

I'm alone. There's a dead bear, and Crystal has her gun, and Dalen just told us that I know the meaning of life. She probably thinks Sunny Days will be mine.

"You weren't really going to shoot me, were you?" I ask. "When we first got the will, back at my trailer."

All of a sudden she starts laughing. "No, brother, but sometimes I want to and pretending makes me feel better. Come on. You can meditate on that later."

We hike a bit in silence.

"Can't believe I shot Dalen," I say. My thigh hurts, but I take that to be a good thing.

Crystal doesn't respond. Keeps walking.

"You think you know it?" she asks as my thigh starts burning. I limp heavily.

"No, not in the way that's going to get me the inheritance," I reply.

"You know what I'm going to do when you get the answer wrong?" she asks. "I'm going to become a hunting guide."

I may not know my meaning of life, but I understand Dalen's. By bringing meaning to the lives of others, he brings it to himself too. That's his meaning, though. Not mine. He'd lost it, and it took Sunny Days to get his mojo back.

The road comes into view and the night air is full of the chop of a rising helicopter.

"There goes a hundred grand," I say.

Before we break back out onto the road, Crystal puts her arm around my shoulder, squeezes once, and then shoves me into the swamp.

Chapter 46

As I stagger out of the swamp, my mother's arms cinch around my chest. My injured thigh muscle cramps from the cold water.

"Idiot. Thought I'd lost another." Her voice breaks, and she swats me in the shoulder and it's then that my leg gives out. I slide down her front to the road. "Ray!" she shouts and tries to lift me. Crystal's there and she drags me along the road to a dry area.

"It's his leg," Crystal explains. "Bear got him."

Four tears bleed through my jeans. The helicopter has been and gone. The place Crystal dragged me to is dry of mud and now I understand why. The bus is gone, too.

"Used all my bandages on the guru," Crystal says.

"Tina's good with the first aid," Salminder says, and I hear her run back into Sunny Days.

I have my pants off by the time she returns. Crystal's cleaned the wound and pronounced that if I want really cool scars I won't bother with stitches.

"Anyone for a midnight burger?" Salminder asks. It's a strange question with me half-naked on the ground, my leg a mess from a grizzly bear. "Tina can help Ray here," he adds.

Tina stands among them, clutching several rolls of bandages and tape.

"Oh, yeah, after a night like that I'll even spring for a Swami Burger," Crystal says, taking the hint. "Nothing I want more than a couple greasy patties and special sauce in my stomach."

"Me, too," my mom replies. She and all the gawking campers follow her, with a sleepy Penny asking why she has to go as well.

Tina rolls her eyes as she kneels at my side. She blanches a little when she sees the claw gashes.

Her hands are gentle as she pours some more peroxide on a cotton ball and dabs it along the edges. They left us alone for a reason, and for the third time in one night, terror rips through me.

"What was it like?" she asks.

"The bear?" She nods, and begins to wrap the wound with clean bandage. "I was so scared," I say. "The thing drooled on me."

"That's pretty gross." She laughs. "Did the meaning of life come to you? Did your life flash before your eyes?"

I look down; what am I supposed to say to her?

"I've read most of Dalen's books, you know? They're pretty good," she says.

"Doesn't it bother you that he steals so many lines from others?"

She glances at me. "No. That makes them better, so why would that bother me?"

We fall back into silence. A sudden urgency squeezes my chest, as though our relationship has been bleeding out for days, and we have between now and when she's done with my leg to bind it. Salminder gave me the gift of alone time with her. What was his message to me? *You're a good man.* And I'm wasting my chance. Just like I seem to have been wasting Dalen's teaching all this time.

"I thought of you," I say. "With the bear. I thought of you."

She stops. A tear drips from her nose to fall on my thigh. She wipes it off.

"Only a seventeen-year-old boy would come up with a girl being the meaning of life," she says. There's a cautious edge to the words that could cut more than any bear claw. But her father's sick. She's protecting herself.

"No," I say. "It's not about sleeping with you. It's about making it right. Us right."

Her twisted smile relaxes. "Sorry," she says. "It's . . . it's been hard. Confusing. I don't want to be alone. I'm not ready yet."

"I'm the one who's sorry. I left you alone!" I say.

But she looks at me with such intensity. "No, don't say that. You were right. You were so right. I would have regretted that night forever." I swallow because I'm not sure what she's saying. "Not because of you," she says, her voice softening. "Because of doing it for the wrong reasons. Wrong time."

"Focus on your dad," I reply, and begin to pull on my pants, but she reaches down to grab my hand.

"I am," she says. "He's going to be okay, they say. No new cancer spots and the ones he has have shrunk. They can't even see them anymore." Her face is radiant even as tears fall.

Now I'm crying, and she abandons the tape to lean down and kiss me, and although it lacks the rush of before, it's the sweeter for it, salty with tears mine and hers.

"You know I don't actually have a million dollars," I say.

"Yeah, I know," she says and kisses me again.

***

There are five more days before I have to tell Sam Peregrine the meaning of life. They are the best five days of my life.

Penny is my sidekick. With my leg I can't fetch cleaning supplies quickly or send messages to campers. Let me say, it's a lot easier having a cute six-year-old ask someone for late payment of rent. While we scrub the floors together, she turns it into a race. Everything becomes a game. Every day she goes swimming. Even while the pool's still cold, and then we warm up around the campfire. There are two fires now. The first fire pit became too small to hold everyone.

At both of them Uncle Jamie sells bags of Grandma's Unicorn Farts, GUFs. He's test-marketing formulations while Penny works on a logo of Grandma riding a unicorn that flies through the air using a jet of rainbows coming from its butt. At the campfires, I watch in amazement as relationships bloom. Jacks go off hand-in-hand while Tina smirks behind her fingers. I'm holding her other hand. Even Obelix has found someone who loves trucks and terriers as much as he does. I wasn't expecting it to be Buck Hawley, but they look really happy together. Salminder's beard has begun to grow back in. For now he looks sort of hip rather than dignified.

Later, my mom officially takes back the camp chores, freeing Tina and me and Penny to begin breaking down the playground and developing plans to build our own. While swinging sledgehammers, we come up with sayings for Swami Burgers.

No burger was ever swallowed in a single bite.

The burger was not. The burger will never be. The burger just is.

To the still mind, the burger surrenders.

Thought leads to action, action to habit, habit to hamburgers.

Knowledge speaks, but burgers listen.

When the student is ready, the burger appears.

And Penny's favorite. *If it's brown, lay down. If it's black, fight back. If it's Swami, fill your tummy.*

I try not to think about the meaning of life. My mom's stopped asking. It's only when I catch her alone that I know something still isn't right. It's hard to say goodbye with Grandma's brain up there.

Crystal's working on logos for her hunting camp, aptly named "The Grizzly" after the taxidermied bear she plans for its entrance. We talk about expanding the trailer park. Standing near the freshly painted gate, I blink in amazement. For once in my lifetime, the camp's name isn't ironic.

On the day I'm to talk to Sam Peregrine, I look in my cracked full-length mirror and see Better-Ray. I don't need to visualize him. He's here. I'm not stronger in the sense that I'm not any more muscular than I was, but there's something in the way I stand that fills out the reflection. It's been more than twenty-one days since this all started, and I've made a habit of it.

My unused climbing gear lies jumbled on the floor. Maybe I'll climb Big Mountain later this summer, but I didn't have to climb anything or go on a vision quest to be better. Everything I needed was all here in front of me. In me.

There's a banging at the door. I open it to Deneze. "Hey,

wanted to wish you luck." He's got his hands in his pockets, and he's staring at his steel-toed boots. "Know what you're going to say?"

"Yeah," I reply. "That—"

"No." He holds up a palm. "Don't tell me, okay? I think that's part of it. It's better if you figure it out on your own."

"Well, I have to tell the executor something," I say.

"Only if you want a million dollars." He laughs.

"How about you? You going to do the vision quest thing?" I ask.

He shakes his head. "Nah." He flushes like he did that time at the pool. "What if I told you I like what I'm doing?"

I realize now that his embarrassment hadn't been because he felt stuck following in his father's footsteps; his embarrassment was because he wanted to follow in them. "I'd say you're really lucky."

"Shouldn't I want something more? I mean, it's garbage disposal."

Deneze isn't the only one who suddenly seems to think I have all the answers. He looks at me with such desperation and uncertainty.

"And other people clean porta-potties." I shrug. "Why do you like it?"

"Well, I'm helping people. I like working on the trucks. I like being outside."

"Sound convincing to me." He nods again and maybe that's all it takes, accepting it. Owning it.

"You want some oatmeal?" I ask. "If you pour enough sugar on top, it's pretty good."

"Gotta finish the route. You going to do Mud and Fire next year, you think?"

"Who knows?"

"Hope so. Want to take it to that townie girl." He grins.

He heads down the path, ponytail bobbing, the richest kid in a hundred miles. But maybe not for long.

A truck honks—Sam Peregrine has arrived.

Chapter 47

My mother hulks at the mouth of the path. She doesn't appear armed but holds her hands tight to her hips. Jaw muscles twitch.

We're like two gunfighters waiting for sundown. I stand with my legs spread, knowing I have to go past her. But I've faced a grizzly. In the dark.

"You know," she says, after half a minute of silence. "I hope you get it right. I never did."

I swallow the lump in my throat. "I killed Grandma." It's out, and I realize that the secret has been tearing at me, holding me back from embracing each moment all month.

"How do you figure?" my mom asks. And I explain the video game that fateful morning. She shakes her head. "Funny. Can't tell you how much your grandma loved being with you. Wasn't killing her. Gave her another thing to live for."

That iceberg in my guts, the last of it, it had split once after the grizzly, and then slowly melted over the rest of the week. I don't feel it anymore. "Thanks, Ma." It's all I can manage to say.

"You can stay, you know, I won't kick you out. And I won't sell, neither," she adds. "But give the meaning a try anyways.

I'm . . . I'm proud of you. Always have been."

As I walk past my mother, I give her a hug. And I rub her back as I lean in to her ear. "I'm kicking you out for sure," I whisper and start laughing, and she laughs with me. "This whole thing is so crazy."

She nods and then shakes her head at Grandma's brain. "It is."

Neither of us really knows what *it* we mean, but that's the point of it. It doesn't matter. There's another honk. Sam's waiting in her truck, waving at us from the road.

I shut her truck door and slump into a chocolate-brown leather seat that smells of pine freshener. She smiles at me, eyes shifting to my mom and then back. In her hand is a letter sealed with wax, and written on it in shaky handwriting is *The Meaning of Life*.

"Why do you and my mother hate each other?" I ask.

Sam glances at the letter and frowns. I realize she wants to see what's in it as much as I do.

"I married her boyfriend," she says. My eyes flicker to her bare ring finger. "He was a bastard. Second-best-looking boy at school, though." Her smile's back. "Sure was cute." She holds up the letter. "Are you ready?" I hesitate. "There's a lot of people who want to know the answer," she says. "Me included."

"But it'll be my grandma's answer," I reply. "I'm not sure my meaning of life's the same as hers. Just like yours wouldn't be my mom's."

On the radio a country singer croons about lost love.

"She was ninety-something," Sam says without missing a step. "Has to have learned a few things." Her fingernail itches at the wax. She's not interested in *my* answer. Not the answer of a seventeen-year-old boy.

"Can I?" I point to the envelope.

"No cheating. I wouldn't want you to peek before giving me your answer." She winks, and I wonder whether she really means it or whether she wants to collude. To take not only the second-best-looking boy at school from her old nemesis, but the inheritance too. After a pause, she hands me the envelope.

"Tell me what you think, Ray—what's the meaning of life?" she asks, without removing her gaze from the envelope's seal.

I shrug and shake my head. With the weight of the wax, the slim envelope feels heavy, even for all that it's supposed to contain. I look again into Sam's shining eyes.

"Well?" she urges. "Aren't you going to try and guess something? Open it!"

I glance out my window.

At the end of the path the sun drapes my trailer, and in the glade stands my mother. She's waiting with a smile on her face. I look to the envelope and back to Sam. "Thank you," I say. "It's not for me to open though. Not for my grandma to answer for me."

An expression of cold fury sweeps over Sam Peregrine, and I jerk her snatching fingers away from the envelope.

"I'm the executor! It's mine to read." I kick open the door, and she screeches again. "Tell me. How do you know?"

In her tight eyes I remember something Dalen said. I don't know what Sam Peregrine's been through. I don't know why she's held tight to bitterness, to the past.

"I can't tell you," I say. "And this won't either."

"The park's your mom's and your uncle's then," she shouts. "There's nothing I can do for you. You'll be thrown out."

"Always was their park. I don't need anything," I say. "It's all here." I tap my head and shut the door.

I take more steps backward, toward my mom. Sam Peregrine sags over the steering wheel of her truck and starts the engine. When she pulls out, my mom appears at my side.

"So?" she asks.

I hold up the letter.

"You didn't open it?"

"I will," I say. "At Grandma's funeral. It's her meaning of life. Not mine."

Her lip quivers, and she closes her eyes. A single tear breaks from her eyelid and tracks down her cheek. I hug her.

"You need to say goodbye, Mom," I say. "We all do."

"That would be nice," she says.

***

The date for the funeral is set for a week later. Over a thousand people show on the day. I think some of them are only here to see me finally crack the wax on the envelope, but many more once stayed in one of the five trailers at the back of the park, trailers I've since sealed with caulking and cleaned. These people, some as old as my grandma, others my mother's age— children of those who have passed but who still carry the stories of Sunny Days—they come with flowers and photos. Memories of a very different legacy than the one I hold of my grandma.

With no body to bury, the ceremony takes place beneath Grandma's brain. A hill of flowers brushes her toes.

When it comes to the eulogy, my mother hints at a lost childhood that wasn't without its good moments. Campfire smoke, songs, marshmallows, and laughter. My uncle talks about magic, the magic of the woods, and his search for it in fireworks, until he finally found it with the help of Grandma. He hands out hundreds of GUFs. I don't care how crazy he seems to everyone; he'll always be the man who carried me away from the jaws of wolves.

Then it's my time. A hush falls over the crowd as I make my way to the front. I touch Grandma's toes and breathe deeply of the fragrant flowers. In my hand's the envelope. Some of the wax has broken away, and it's dirty with my fingerprints. But I haven't opened it. My stomach twists as I do, the heat of expectations, the wax falling to the grass. Inside's a single sheet, which I unfold and read.

"It's a recipe," I say. "It's a recipe for apple pie. The meaning of life is baked apple pie."

Maybe she was celebrating a bit too much when she wrote her will. But a recipe's as good as any. Those in the audience who once stayed here and shared in Grandma's pie, they smile knowingly. They understand even if most the people in attendance simply lift an eyebrow and shake their head at an old coot.

The letter generates a titter of laughter and more than a few groans. Everyone starts launching unicorn farts. I duck out of the way. As the GUFs flare off of her statue's boobs, I'm pretty sure she's smiling in her brain. My uncle's eyes shine with more than tears, and he grins at me with each pop of a fart. Between his thumb and forefinger he dangles one. He waggles it and points at Grandma's statue. My jaw unhinges and he gleefully whips another fart into her chest.

I get it, suddenly: the weeklong fire. The white-hot kiln in the woods. That's where Grandma had gone. Uncle Jamie had cremated her, and now the ashes are sprinkled in the farts. She's part of GUF's secret recipe. I laugh as I throw my GUF into the air. It lands in my palm where it flashes green.

"Bye, Grandma," I say and let the wind take her away.

***

A week later I receive a note from Dalen. In it, he sends a check for $5000, a refund for one week of mentoring less medical expenses, including the airlift. I offer it to my mom and to my uncle, but they tell me to keep the money, so I split it with Crystal.

I read the note aloud to Tina:

> *Ray, here's everything I've learned. Some of it from you, my friend. Yes, I even stand on your shoulders.*
>
> *Every journey may begin with a single step. But the path is not set and each step is a choice. Don't let the goal become more important than the step. Your goal will change. Your values will guide you, be true to them, but make choices at each fork that benefit others as much as yourself.*
>
> *The meaning of the adventure will be based on the spirit with which you take these steps. A path of joy is a joyful life. A path of bitterness or longing will lead to a path full of brambles and thorns. But no matter your age*

or circumstance, you will always have your whole life ahead of you. Each day the journey begins anew.

The easiest way to be joyful is to bring joy. Your grandma lost sight of that at the end, but your mother is finding that path where your grandma left off, thanks to her gift to you all. The meaning of life is weighed at every root and stone. It is uphill, and downhill. The path does not care how long it is. It is the path.

Find your meaning by trying things and being attuned to what makes you happy. Set goals. Visualize them. Stay positive. Persevere—it takes time. Focus on your strengths and acknowledge, but do not dwell on, your weaknesses. Celebrate regularly. Every step.

The only missteps will come—and they will come—when you stop believing in your own meaning. When you will choose to see the negative, the failure, and compare yourself to others, often when you know very little about what you're comparing yourself to.

It is your game. Your rules. Be sure to make it yours and give it your all. But like any good game, it shouldn't be taken too seriously. And it isn't winner takes all. Because the prize is an illusion of your own creation—never forget that. While you're playing, lift up everyone you can around you, even if they have disappointed you. The people you play the game with are as important as the game itself. You will need them as much as they need you. Let forgiveness into your heart; assume that everyone's day was at least as difficult as your own.

Ray, people speak of the glass being half-full or half-

empty. Wise people know two things. That the glass is always full and that glass, Ray, that glass is a beautiful glass.

Above the edge of the note, Tina's eyes shimmer. Around the knot in my throat, I say, "Pretty sure I've seen this posted on Facebook."

"Me too." She laughs, and then smiles at me. "Doesn't make it wrong."

"No," I agree. "Not wrong at all."

Epilogue

A few years later Dalen comes to town and asks if I'll join him on stage and tell my story. By this time, the camp has three parts: Grizzlies, run by my sister. My mom's section, the Apple Pie Club, a camp for people who need it. And I operate Sunny Days, for jacks and everyone else. It now features a popular gaming trailer, and I offer a once a season excursion to Big's peak—it's not such a hard climb after all. Every year we host the largest truck and ATV charity rally in the area. Every year Obelix comes back to head it up. Our million-dollar camp's worth more now. How much? Priceless, I guess. I don't really care.

Uncle Jamie left. He needed a warehouse to ship all his fireworks from. Grandma's ashes are spreading all over the world.

Tina and I broke up at the end of the first summer, but we're still friends. She's in university, studying to be a doctor. Salminder's cancer's in remission. He runs Swamiburger and uses the fortunes we made up with Penny on the wrappers. I'm a summertime big brother to Penny and that's pretty awesome, too. *When the teacher is ready, the student appears.*

The crowd at Dalen's talk is thin, but his energy is enough to light a stadium.

"I'm not going to talk to you about homeless turned millionaires." Dalen begins his spiel, and Charlie adjusts the sound level. "Or billionaires who regained the love of their families. I could. But I won't. What I want to do, is to tell you the story of an ordinary kid. A kid named Ray, who was given an extraordinary opportunity to find the meaning of life."

There's clapping as I climb onto the stage. Dalen grips me in a back-bending hug.

It's funny, I'm really proud of myself. I run a happy camp. I've faced a grizzly. But as Dalen hands me the microphone, there's still a little bit of barf in my throat.

I must be doing something right. I begin.

"Here's what killed Grandma."

Acknowledgements

The more I write, the more I acknowledge that my writing is a product of my reading, of heard podcasts, of listening to people, of working with and being a part of a community. It doesn't come from my imagination; it comes from the tinder of what goes into my imagination. I can't possibly thank everyone who has touched my life or even this book, but I want to express my gratitude in general for philosophers, gurus of all types, and intellectuals who pursue answers to some of life's most challenging questions.

I do have a multitude of people without whom this book would not have happened. Thank you to Stephanie Parent, Joshua Johnson, Catherine Adams, Carrie Cuinn, Polgarus Studios, Jason & Marina Anderson, Glendon Haddix, Martin Stiff at Amazing15 for the cover, the Odyssey Writers Workshop, the Sunnyside Writers Group, and Gina Panettieri. I stand on all of your shoulders.

I dedicated this book to my elder daughters because I wrote it for them and was inspired to write it for them. Young adults face great societal and personal challenges. I don't pretend this book has answers, after all most of it comes from internet memes, but I do hope this story will help my daughters realize that their answers are waiting, whenever they are ready to search for them.

Finally, to my wife, my pillar and life. Thank you. If all we need is one person to believe in us, then I'm lucky indeed.

Thank you, dear Reader. May you all live with a little bit of vomit in your mouth.

If you enjoyed this book and would like to review it, please do, wherever you make purchases. There are no greater gifts to an author than reviews and word of mouth.

You can find me on Amazon, Goodreads, Facebook, and Twitter. I love to talk.

If you'd like to hear about new releases and take part in giveaways or opportunities to act as an advance reader, please sign up to my newsletter on my website or via my Facebook page. You'll get a free book. ☺

About the Author

Michael is an award winning author who lives in Ottawa, Canada. His graphic novels, novels, and early readers have been published by Rubicon Publishing and distributed by Pearson Education, Scholastic, and Oxford University Press. To learn more about Michael and his projects, visit his website at www.michaelfstewart.com.

CPSIA information can be obtained
at www.ICGtesting.com
Printed in the USA
FSHW02n2030300418
47647FS